library

LOVELY

Rin Sangar

NFB
Buffalo, New York

Copyright © 2025 Rin Sangar

Printed in the United States of America

Lovely/Sangar—1st Edition

ISBN: 979-8-9990851-6-0

Fiction> Gothic
Fiction> Horror>Gothic
Fiction> Suspense
Fiction> Supernatural>American Gothic

This is a work of fiction. All characters are fictitious. Any resemblance to actual events or locations, unless specified, or persons, living or dead is entirely coincidental.

No part of this book may be reproduced or transmitted in any form by any means, electronic or mechanical, including photocopying, recording, or by any information storage and retrieval system without permission in writing by the author.

NFB Publishing
119 Dorchester Road
Buffalo, New York 14213
For more information visit Nfbpublishing.com

For Sophia, who I wrote my first stories for.
And for Trey, who read more drafts of this than any one person should.
Thank you.

Lovely

Chapter One

It was early summer, the kind where the sun knew spring was over but the humidity had yet to catch on, and the town of Lovely was enjoying an evening so peaceful even the crickets couldn't disturb it. Local historians claimed the name came from the only word that English colonists could muster after the view of the lake lapping at the roots of the sycamore trees at sunset knocked them speechless - but Jennifer, the twenty-one year old waitress at the only diner in town, claimed it was a misspelling of Lonely. Dusk was claiming the town, the dirt roads and crabgrass fading to a murky black, shop registers counted and closed, porch lights switched off as the front door locked, weak street lights illuminating local election signs. The last of the inhabitants were going home, and even the kids known for unlatching windows and prying open screen doors decided it was better to stick to phone calls and scandalous magazines tonight, and to save the outside world for Friday. Tonight, the streets could rest easy, troubled only by possums and raccoons and other creatures of the night. Tomorrow morning, a child's dead body will rise up from the depths of the lake, pale and bloated. Tomorrow afternoon, a city cab will carry Heather Strand back into town after a three month absence. Tomorrow everything would change - but for tonight, there was a moment of blissful ignorance hanging in the air.

Heather tipped her head back, resting on the worn leather car seat her sneakers had already left scuff marks on, and debated jumping out of the moving vehicle as she gazed out at the countryside speeding by. The cab driver shot her a dirty look, and in any other circumstance he would probably have said something or even stopped the car and demanded she get out, but instead he just simply kept glowering from under two salt and pepper eyebrows. One of the perks of a recent discharge from a state psychiatric facility.

The cab turned onto the main street of Lovely, a two mile long stretch of sun bleached stones that used to boast a tourist industry and now could barely claim a dozen stores. Then it was a right turn, five minutes of crunching gravel, then a left, driving straight over a dirt hill and fifteen short minutes until a dead stop. Heather shoved the door open, grabbed the stained brown backpack on the seat next to her and clambered out, murmuring a "thanks" that didn't stop her from slamming the door. The cab couldn't speed off fast enough - paid in advance, no reason sticking around in Lovely any longer than you had to. She understood.

The house in front of her - one floor, slanted roof, brown paint flaking off - loomed in a way she hadn't expected it to. Red sneakers forced themselves over more dirt than grass patches and tree roots. Her hand, chipped nail polish and fake metal rings, forced open the door handle - which didn't open.

"Huh." She dug through the backpack, dragging out a brass key attached to a roughed-up toy rabbit. Key in the lock, turn- it doesn't turn. "Fuck."

Heather made her way around the house, eyeing the trees surrounding her on three sides. There was sap solidifying in the heat, ants crawling up and down the splintering bark. As a kid she used to think the trees would stretch on forever, and she could just keep walking until everything was *behind*. Now she knew the border of the trees was a mere mile away, stopping in a jagged line behind a liquor store.

The back door opened, swinging into a kitchen that was all pale green linoleum and yellow tile. Heather pushed the door shut, dumping her backpack on the notched wooden chair closest to her, and meeting her father's eyes. For a brief second, her mind flashed through what she looked like - light brown roots peeking through black hair that hung in lanky strands down her back, eye bags, charcoal sweater one size too big, gauze on her forearms - and then she snapped back to him. Stubble on his chin, grease stains on his t-shirt, fury in his eyes.

"Hi." The word caught in her throat.

"New key's on the coffee table. Don't be out past six." He stood, dropping a mug into the sink so loudly she was surprised it didn't shatter.

"Dad, I-"

"Heading out. Got to be at Henderson's."

"Henderson? Why-"

"Their kid was found in the lake this morning."

Heather's heart dropped. "Tyler?"

"No, Max. Stay away from them."

"Stay away from-"

"I'm late." He walked past her. She heard the scrape of the latch, the turning of two different locks, the door slam. He'd taken the air out of the room with him.

Her room was exactly as she had left it. Bed unmade, schoolbooks strewn loose, dirty cups gathering mould and dust. Heather forced the window open, letting the afternoon heat roll in. The lace curtains still had an ashy char on the hems, the one flower in an old glass soda bottle was dead, her shelves still gathering dust.

She pulled open the drawer of her bedside table - light wood, old, part of a matching set with her bed frame and desk - and reached under it to the razor blade taped there. Then she pulled open her closet door, sifting through school uniforms and loose sweaters and men's shirts until she found the dress from her fifth birthday. Light blue fabric, tulle skirt, ribbons and flowers, heart shaped pockets on the bodice. Half a carton of cigarettes in one pocket, a lighter in the other.

Half an hour later and Heather was on the threadbare orange couch in the living room, television running a comedy, a glass of whiskey sat on the coffee table. Her hands trembled as she used the razor edge to slice strips through the gauze, wincing as she peeled it off her skin, the lit cigarette in her mouth drawing circles of smoke. The bandages started at her wrists, snaking and writhing up both arms to her elbows. She threw them into the kitchen trash, dumping a stack of unfinished assignments on top - no point in keeping bad notes for a year she was retaking anyway. Cigarette finished, she pulled open the fridge, snapped open a container of leftover soup, poured it down the sink drain. Left the stained plastic tub in the sink.

Seven years ago. It was the dead of night, and the deputy, Ben Ritter, had his feet up on the desk and a newspaper in his hands, the radio humming, the sheriff securely in his office. The night had been quiet, knock on wood, and hopefully he could get home before five a.m.. If he did, he could wake up early enough to go to that sandwich shop he liked before his next shift. All the delights of working nights.

He reached for his rapidly cooling cup of coffee, shaking the blond hair out of his eyes. He needed a haircut. The sip he took was more biting than he thought it would be, but he swallowed it down, wondering if it was worth wheeling out the small office television and booting up a film. The door slammed open.

Ben flinched into position, his back straight, one hand reaching for his holster. There was a young girl in the doorway, brown hair falling into her sweaty face, drowning in a t-shirt for a rock band he didn't recognise, her feet bare. She couldn't have been older than nine or ten.

"Hello," he blurted out, his mind racing. "Come on in. How can I help?"

The kid walked in. He could see the scratches on her arms and legs, the goosebumps on her skin. Her eyes shifted to the door behind him.

"I need help," she said, matching his gaze with a steady sight. "I think- I think my mum's hurt."

He finally found it in himself to force a soft smile. "Why do you think that, sweetie?"

For a moment, he saw the light in her eyes darken. A flash of something sinister. "I saw my dad shoot her."

Ben's smiled dropped, his skin prickling instinctively. "Let me grab the sheriff, honey."

He made it to the office door without stumbling. Normally he would knock - but tonight, he pushed it open, stepping in. "Sheriff? We have an emergency. I think you should take this."

The sheriff's face didn't change, the same levelled expression he always wore. "Bring her in."

Ben nodded, relief running through his veins. "Of course."

He held the door open, his mouth dry. He couldn't say anything. The kid walked past him.

Ben sank back down into his chair, just before he collapsed into it. They were in there, the two of them, for four hours. He kept telling himself, *just five more minutes* and then he would go home. He stayed until the kid walked past him, pushing open the door and her silhouette fading into the woods. He didn't say goodnight to the sheriff.

"Fucking idiot." Heather stood in front of the phone, television off, third glass of whisky in hand. A few hours of restlessness had passed - it feels like aeons. The stained lace of the doily the phone sat on taunted her, the cracked plastic of the handle mocking, the trestle table sagging under the weight. There was a fly buzzing somewhere in the room. She squeezed her eyes shut, grabbed the receiver, dialled by memory.

Two rings. Then, a guy's voice, young, tired, familiar. "Hello?"

Heather didn't expect him. Her knuckles on the glass whiten.

"Hello?" His voice, still. *Tyler.*

Say something.

"If this is a prank, I'll kill you."

"I'm back." Heather's voice was barely a whisper.

Click.

The receiver floated down from her hand and back onto the phone. The whisky drained, her feet pacing circles on the wooden floor. It was late, seven, the sun beginning to set. Heather flicked on the fluorescent bulbs, z yellow glow lighting up the dust collecting on what counted for family photos-

Ring.

She froze, eyes scanning to the locked front door.

Ring.

She knew it was the phone. She knew she was home alone. She knew she wasn't moving.

Ring.

Heather lunged for the phone, hitting her knee hard on the coffee table. Wincing, she picked up the receiver, phone jammed against her ear. Held her breath.

There was a moment of silence, heart pounding in her ears, fingers gripping the plastic.

"Meet me at the bridge at midnight."

Thirty years ago. "When Joe first started working at the Sheriff's office, he had lived in Lovely for just under a week. He'd been fired from the firehouse two towns over for excessive use of force during a false alarm, and he was looking for a new line of work. The Sheriff's office suited him nicely - he liked his coworkers, he liked the hours, he liked how he looked in the uniform. He was fortunate enough to stop a teenager driving recklessly, who just so happened to be the culprit behind a string of burglaries, earning him the rank of detective. Joe was the Sheriff's rising star, taken under his wing and primed to lead the force one day.

Then about six months later, Joe was working on this case for about a week. Three missing kids, parents worried, no current leads. He was holed up in the station for hours at a time, living off the coffee pot, sticking maps onto the wall and leafing through arrest records going back fifty years. And there's this one night where it's just him and the Sheriff left in the office, and it's already dark outside, and Joe's had a couple of stiff drinks. They start working together on this case, rehashing the details, pouring over what they know. Joe keeps the drinks coming, strong ones, and the Sheriff's putting them away without blinking. Effects of the job.

Now, Joe's tolerance is pretty high, so he's just a little more relaxed and maybe a little more creative. But the Sheriff is not a drinker, to his newest detective's surprise, and his speech is getting more and more slurred. He's going off topic, talking about similar cases from years ago, disappearances from other towns over, about his first case as the Sheriff. He's talking about his life before he was Sheriff. He's talking years back.

Now, I don't know what he said. But what I do know is Joe forced himself to keep calm for another half hour, and then he wished the Sheriff a good night and left the station. He got into his car and he started driving - drove right past his house, over the bridge out of Lovely, drove straight over the state lines. Apparently he lives on the west coast now, in some big city, working the morning shift at a diner. I heard that, to this day, he keeps a loaded shotgun under the counter in case anyone from Lovely ever walks in."

Chapter Two

It's past eleven when her father gets home. Heather's already curled up under her sheets, door left open on purpose, hallway light illuminating her back. She hears him stumble through the house, hears the liquor cabinet open and slam, hears the television blare on. A moment of silence. Then there's a shadow in her doorway, swaying and wafting malt into her room. Heather squeezes her eyes closed.

"You awake?"

He's slurring, his voice hoarse. He's probably been with the Henderson's all afternoon - which includes the home bar set up in their basement.

"You're asleep. I'll see you in the morning, I guess."

Heather counts her breaths.

"It's weird having you home."

In, out. In, out.

"You should be dead."

In, out. She doesn't even hear it. This is happening in a film, this isn't about her. She's an observer on the outside.

Heather's dad straightens up, the doorframe groaning in relief, and stumbles down the hallway. She hears the slam of his door, then the dull thump of his body hitting a mattress, then a snore.

She sits up in bed, joints aching. Heather pulls on a navy pair of jeans, belting them to her waist, a big knitted black sweater, some beat up sneakers. She loads her pockets with cigarettes, a lighter, a pack of gum and her shiny new house key. She opens the window and shimmies out, feet hitting the dirt. It's still a little warm out, enough for the sweater to keep her from shivering, staving the cold from her bones. There aren't a lot of stars out.

Twenty minutes later and she's approaching the bridge. It's not much - just wooden railings where a dirt road crosses a river, with a single streetlight basking it in a warm glow. The kind of place where your parents may have carved their initials in the wood between chaste kisses. Not as exciting as Beatrice's expansive garden shed and its flow of stashed beer.

He's there, of course. Heather doesn't think he's ever been less than five minutes early, never mind late. Tyler Henderson leans on the wooden railing, hair golden in the lamp's glow, denim jacket collar turned up. He's holding a beer bottle, his heavy leather boots scuffing lines in the dirt.

Heather steps into the streetlight. "Hey."

He startles, and she feels bad.

"You're back." His voice is empty, lifeless. He takes another swig of beer.

She leans against the railing with him. "Yeah. Sorry I was gone so long."

"Don't fucking apologise." He's using his gruff voice, the scary one he uses when someone tries to talk over him. She tenses. Allows it to hang in the air.

"They found him this morning."

"What happened?" She's heard the rumours, obviously, that things were bad at home, that his brother was bullied at school, that the younger sibling took the next bus out of here.

Tyler lets out a long sigh. "Max went missing just after you left, like, March? Just didn't come home from school one day. Not like him. And we searched, everywhere, every inch of the town. Me and my dad spent hours walking through the woods yelling his name. And nothing, and I know I should expect it but they found him this morning. Just in the lake, face down, drained of blood. He's gone. And everyone, the doctor and the medic and the coroner, are saying they don't know what happened. Like it doesn't make sense."

Heather swallows hard. "I'm-"

"If you say you're sorry, I'll punch you in the face."

She lets out a dry laugh. He stares off into the difference and she fishes a cigarette out of her pocket, placing it in her mouth and searching for her lighter.

"Stop." Tyler pulls the cigarette out of her mouth, tucking it behind his ear. He hates that she smokes. She hates that he doesn't look at her in the hallways at school.

"What do you think happened to your brother?" It comes out meaner than she thought it would, but she did think it would be a little mean.

"What happened to you in March?"

"You don't want to hear about that." Heather plucks the cigarette from behind his ear, lighting it before he has the chance to speak any more. She blows the exhale in his face, burning up her lungs, laughing as he winces.

The two of them stare up at the night sky for a moment. There are very few stars you can see over Lovely - less a case of light pollution, more of a case of a town that wants to crush the hope out of you.

"I can't do this," Heather says, at the same time as Tyler says "I need your help."

"What?"

"What?"

"What did you say?"

"I said I need your help, what did you say?"

"Just that, you know, I feel like shit."

It's barely a convincing lie. She's honestly running on empty here. She is very lucky that an instant look of worry creases his brow.

"Oh, I'm sorry. I can walk you home, or give you a ride, or-"

"No, no, I'm fine. What did you need help with?"

Tyler frowns at her. "I'm still trying to figure that out. I'll call you tomorrow, okay?"

"Okay," Heather nods. She finishes her cigarette as he downs his beer. "I should go."

"You sure you don't want me to walk you?" There's a light behind his grey eyes, some gleam of wanting to be helpful, to look after someone. It disgusts her.

"No, I'm good. Call me tomorrow?"

"Okay."

Heather stubs out her cigarette, gives him a nod and heads off into the darkness, leaving him in the little beam of artificial sunlight he's claimed for himself.

She's halfway home when she takes a sharp turn off the dirt road, shuffling through grass and ferns. Heather leans her back against a tree, sap staining her sweater, looking up at the night sky. His brother was found dead this morning. No one has an answer. He asked if she was okay.

Her hands fumble with her belt, snapping it open and ripping open the button and zips of her jeans. She pushes one hand down, under the cotton of her underwear, and the next fifteen minutes are filled with her biting moans into her night.

Roughly forty years ago, Lucy Miller worked in the town archives, which was the rather grandiose title given to the damp basement of the Sheriff's office. Her job was to show up five minutes early, make a pot of coffee which she wouldn't touch, organise the mess of newspapers and editorials and journals rotting in the archives, and not flinch when someone mentioned the tightness of her sweater or the length of her skirt. She enjoyed skimming through articles, categorising them by year and whether they pertained to *crime* or *town events* or *local news* or *other*. In just six years, which was a lightning speed for a town such as Lovely, she'd turned the paper pit that was the basement into a neatly filed and organised stack of shelves, as well as creating a categorising system to expedite the process.

She came into work on an unusually bright November morning, all long polka dot skirt and red sweater with matching gloves, hair curled and eyes sparkling. Tomorrow was the seventh year anniversary of her first day at the archives, and she had arranged to pick up a cake on her way home to bring in and mark the occasion. She was also considering beginning efforts to make a time capsule - she could get the school to contribute, and some of the more enthusiastic locals, and hide it down in the basement to be opened in a hundred years by, say, an eager town archivist who would write fictional tales about the whirlwind life of the brash individual who started it all. A girl could dream.

Lucy picked up the stack of post left precariously by the coffee maker, put on a fresh pot, and headed downstairs. The single exposed bulb cast light on her desk, dressed up in a pink tablecloth with a lace hem and adorned with a collection of sketches of her cat. She sat down and began sifting through the day's news, scissors ready to clip out any story that seemed of note.

> *Winner of the town spelling bee crowned. Unseasonably warm weather for this time of year. Church fete draws record crowds. Child found dead on the side of the road, bloodless. Five hairstyles to make him swoon. Sixteen year old presumed runaway found gutted in the woods. New! recipe for jello ham. Baseball game ends-*

Lucy paused, looking at the articles she'd just cut out. She spread them over the table, smoothing out the creases. Something felt off.

The coffee! She was back upstairs, pulling the grounds out of the machine before the smell could linger. She used a cloth to wipe down the coffee rings already staining the counter, and reached for a mug with one shaky hand.

"Sweetheart?"

Why was she worried? The crisis had been averted. There was no reason for her to still be shaking.

"Lucy?"

She jumped, turning around. The Sheriff stood behind her, uniform immaculately pressed, badge glinting in the light, day-old stubble littering his chin. He eyed her, polite concern creasing his brow.

"You alright?"

"Yes! Yes, of course. I just spaced for a moment," Lucy fumbled up, feeling her cheeks get hot.

"You don't normally drink coffee, huh?"

Lucy looked down. The mug in her hand was half drunk, and there was a bitter taste coating her tongue. "Just trying something new," she managed, panic rising in her throat. "Excuse me."

She hurried back downstairs, legs shaky on the stairs. The coffee mug was leaving a damp brown ring on the centre of the church fete article, but Lucy was pulling files from thirteen years ago, and twenty six years ago, and thirty nine, all in red binders for *crime*. She leafed through, wanting desperately to be wrong.

Thirty nine years ago. June 18th, six year old Bobby is found in an outfield, dead and pale. August 26th, eighteen year old Mary is found floating face down in a river, and when they turn her over her abdomen has been hollowed out. November 3rd, Mark, loving father and husband, drives his car into a tree during a thunderstorm and dies.

Twenty six years ago. June 1st, nine year old Annie falls asleep and doesn't wake up. August 15th, thirteen year old George's torso is on the bridge, presumably due to coyotes or lions. November 29th, Stanley who ran the butchers carved his wrists open with his own paring knife.

Thirteen years ago. June 5th, three year old Bobby-Sue was found in her crib, dead in her sleep. August 30th, sixteen year old Margaret falls out of her high school locker, organs ripped out. November 12th, the school janitor known only as Stan hangs himself in the same hallway.

Six months ago, an unidentified five year old's body was found on the side of the road, drained of blood. Two months ago, sixteen year old Melony was found dead in the edges of the woods surrounding Lovely - her body had been identified a week ago. Today was November 1st.

Lucy's hands shook over the scattering of newspaper clippings, staring down at the floor. She wasn't exactly a detective, but this certainly seemed like a pattern. A serial killer, perhaps, or kind of twisted tradition - surely not a coincidence. She should go upstairs, find the Sheriff, relay all this-

"Lucy?"

A voice on the stairs. Her head snapped up, seeing the Sheriff stood there, a look of polite worry on his face.

"That's quite a mess you're making there, huh?"

"Sorry," she forced out, seeing the sheaths of newspaper that had been ripped off of the shelves in her desperate search. "I'll get it reorganised."

"I'm sure you will, sweetheart," the Sheriff smiled, already moving on to his next thought. "Would you be a dear and run out to get some of those sandwiches that I like for lunch?"

"Yes, of course," Lucy's feet were numb, moving across the basement and to the stairs. Her hands hadn't stopped shaking.

"Get yourself something too." The Sheriff pressed a crisp note into her hand, almost folding her fingers around it. She watched him head up the stairs, tongue twisted.

An hour later and Lucy was sat back at her desk, one hand holding a rye bread sandwich, the other steadily filing newspaper clippings into their assigned folders. A strawberry milkshake with extra cream - her childhood favourite - sat next to her, condensation and milk dripping onto her tablecloth and gloves and a couple of too-close articles.

At 5 p.m. sharp that night, Lucy turned off the light in the basement, wished the station a good night, and began the ten minute walk home. On the way, she stopped at the bakery for a slice of cherry cake, and then at the diner for a burger and two pieces of apple pie. The sun was beginning to set when she unlocked the door to her one bedroom apartment, nestled on top of the florist on main street. Lucy opened a can of soda from the fridge, wrapped herself in a blanket crochet by her grandmother, turned on the television. She then nestled herself onto the couch with a pint of ice cream, a large glass of white wine and a bottle of sleeping pills. Bathed in the golden glow of the setting sun, she finished the bottle of pills, her feet propped up on the lace covering her coffee table. Her last thoughts were of vanilla ice cream and talk show hosts.

Lucy's body was found four days later, when her neighbour became suspicious of the smell. The sheriff's office never hired another archivist.

It's past noon when Heather wakes the next morning, shivering under her blanket, hair a rat's nest. She stumbles to the bathroom, turning the shower on as hot as it will go. Waiting until the steam means she can't see the hollowness of her eyes in the mirror.

Twenty minutes later, skin rubbed raw and clumps of hair forced down the drain, she's in the kitchen fighting with the cupboards. Her dad's already at work, despite it being a Sunday, a pot of burnt coffee the only indicator he was home at all. She settles on a glass of orange juice, lacing it with whiskey.

Ring.

Heather makes it to the phone in record time, almost knocking it off the table in her haste to pick it up. She jams the receiver against her ear and of course it's him.

"Did I wake you?"

"No," Heather tries to subtly cough the sleep out of her throat.

"Okay. My parents are out for the day. Wanna come over?"

Goosebumps ripple up her arms. It's not exactly like she has any prior commitments.

"Give me twenty minutes."

Thirty minutes later and Heather is loitering in his kitchen, watching Tyler pour cereal into a bowl. The last time she was in this house, she was ten years old with a whole world waiting for her and a house that didn't feel like a mausoleum. It's one of those things.

"You wanna go upstairs?" He asks between slurping spoonfuls.

"Sure."

The stairs are mahogany, a red carpet running up the middle. There are polished photos on the wall - Tyler winning a spelling bee medal, Max's first day of school, the whole family in matching pyjamas on Christmas. Heather digs her nails into her palms.

His room is larger than her living room, all band posters and neatly stacked school books and vinyls ordered by colour. He sets the bowl of cereal on his organised desk, flopping down on the bed that she thinks is larger than her whole future. Heather hovers, discomfort rising in her throat.

"How are you?"

It should be her asking that question. This isn't fair.

"I'm fine. How are you?"

Tyler shrugs, rolling onto his back. His sage green polo shirt rides up a little as he tucks his hands behind his head, grey eyes trained on the ceilings.

"It's hard, but I would be worried if it wasn't," he says carefully. "I think I'm alright, all things considered."

"That's good," Heather leans on his desk, resisting the urge to scour the pile of books closest to her.

"I would be better if you joined me."

She looks up and his eyes are glued to her, that almost puppy dog look that he knows works on her. She wants to be angry. Instead, she rips her laces undone, kicking off her shoes. Heather settles on the bed next to him, two inches between them, arms crossed over her stomach. She's grateful she wore a burgundy sweater that grazes her thighs and thick denim jeans.

Lying down next to him, shoulders on the soft blue quilt of his bed, Heather has to stop herself from dreaming. No one's happy in Lovely. Searching for it is a special brand of fruitless.

"I missed you." Tyler's voice is soft, gentle. He skates his fingertips over her wool clad shoulder.

"I know," she whispers back. "I would've called. They didn't let me."

"Where were you?" He's propped up on one elbow, looking down on her. It's a dangerous angle. One move of his right hand and she would be trapped, pinned between him and the beautiful quilt, at the mercy of his breath on her neck-

"Where do you think?"

Tyler shrugs. "Everyone at school had a different story. Someone said you were sick, someone said you'd dropped out, someone said you were staying with your mum. I just figured you skipped town for a bit and you'd come back when you were ready."

Heather smiled wryly. "I wish."

"Tell me what happened?"

"I don't-"

He's closer, hand on her shoulder, eyes pleading. "Please tell me. Max is gone and everyone's lying to me about it. I need you to be honest."

Heather swallowed, hard. His brother's death isn't her fault. Someone should take responsibility. "I was in a hospital, upstate. Kind of a psychiatric ward."

"What are you, crazy?" He half laughed.

She shook her head. "No, not crazy. I just don't want to be here."

Fuck. More honest than she meant to be.

"I'm glad you're here."

Heather wished she could believe him. She also wished he didn't start kissing her, and that his hand didn't slide up under her sweater, and that he didn't whisper he loved her just before he finished.

In his defence, Tyler remembered a lot for three months of forced abstinence. He remembered that she liked to keep her sweater on, and not to be offended when she covered her eyes, and to bite her neck but not leave marks. Seven out of ten, plus two for the added effort he put in. An A.

"We need to figure out what happened to Max." Tyler said, his head on her shoulder, his arms wrapped around her. He was still naked, his clothes strewn around the bed, one hand drawing circles over her hip.

"Okay." Heather nodded. "You going to school tomorrow?"

"Yeah."

"Don't."

"Okay."

"There's a strange feeling that sometimes hits you when you live in a small town, where the nearest bus to the next city is somehow always an hour away and there are empty days that stretch ahead with no one on the other end of the phone. It's the kind of feeling that wakes you up in the middle of the night and keeps you in your bed, convinced that *it* is in the hallway just outside your door. The vague thought that when you look out into the woods outside of your house, the woods look back.

Of course, there are those who argue that the woods *are* looking back at you. Usually children, or the clinically insane, but that doesn't mean you should discard their two cents. There used to be an English teacher at the high school - Heather had him, probably, for a year or two - who fully believed it. He'd moved to Lovely after being fired from a professor position at his alma mater, because his car ran out of gas a mile outside the town limits, and he'd had such a nice slice of pie at the town diner he had settled here for good. If you stayed behind class a little too long, or if the topic of discussion even slightly edged in that direction, he would tell you about the woods. Several hundred years ago, before the trees were hacked down from the town centre and the houses built and roads carved into the ground, the woods were wild and filled with plants and animals and something *else*. That something else would imitate and mimic, take the form of raccoons and vultures and snakes, blend in with the wildlife; not perfectly, but closely enough. And then the people came, and forced back the trees, and changed the habitat, and became the apex predators. And the things in the woods saw this, and did what they had been doing for a millenia. They mimicked.

Firstly, they would stay in the woods. That's what they knew, and when the humans did come out that far, they usually came alone and vulnerable. But the years passed, and they got braver. They started venturing into Lovely, under the cover of night, when the streets were harder to see and anything could be blamed on shadows. And then they got braver still, and they came during the day. They got used to mimicking better and better, hiding in plain sight. And one day, one of them walked up to a house, opened the front door, sat down at the dinner table and ate a meal with a family. With its family. After that, I doubt they ever left."

Twenty minutes later, after Tyler had fallen asleep and Heather had painstakingly slowly wiggled out from under him, she was sat at his desk, rooting through his drawers. She wasn't trying to snoop, it was just *so* easy. He had old baseball tickets, a faded yearbook, polaroids of himself, some other girl's panties. The bottom drawer wasn't closed all the way - she shoved it shut. It jammed. Heather kept her eyes on the steady rise and fall of Tyler's bare chest, comforter around his hips, as she reached over the sheaths of old notes and past the back of the drawer. She pulled out a navy, spiral-bound hardcover notebook, with the words *keep out* scrawled on the front in Tyler's handwriting. She shouldn't look.

The first six pages were basic accounts of his school days - which of his friends was dating the other, what assignments he had due, the teachers he hated. She flicked through, hoping to find something highlighted for importance or his brother's name or her's; there was hers.

The entry was dated March 20th, two weeks after she had *left* - for lack of a better word - town, just over three months ago from today. It was about half a page, mostly about the English essay he had due and the lab report for his chemistry class, both of which she doubted he did. There was a line about how he'd gotten to second base with Beatrice on the stairwell outside the gym during lunch, *gross*, and then the very last sentence. "Heather's gone, miss her." The 'miss' was underlined twice.

Heather pushed it back behind the drawer, getting up and stretching. She grabbed the pack of cigarettes she'd stashed behind a dusty photo of Tyler aged six, holding the lead of his old dog for the first time. The door closed softly behind her and she left through the back garden gate, waiting until she was over the ditch and in the sparse woodland before lighting up and exhaling into the early evening. Tyler, who hadn't been woken up by any of these closing doors, but by her moving away from him, sat up in bed. He leaned against the windowsill, watching her make her way home alone. One of these days he would drive her home, he told himself for the thousandth time.

It was a warm afternoon, normal for June, and she was in the nicer part of town, where the teachers and store managers lived. She had to fight the urge to throw a rock through a couple of the windows, especially those with pools in the back and neatly manicured lawns, but it was an easy walk back. This was the farthest she had walked in the last three months, she realised, and she could feel it in her calves. The more she walked, the smaller the houses got, the roads more uneven, the lawns more weeds than grass. Heather passed the last still-lit streetlight, and fifteen minutes later was rounding into her own drive, all the lights in the house off. Her key unlocked the front door, she tracked dirt down the hall to her room, and she was asleep within the hour.

Two or three years ago. Mary-Beth was four hours into the nine hour drive back from dropping her daughter off for her first year of college. The tears had stopped three and a half hours ago, and had been replaced by bickering with Ted and flipping through the faded magazines in the glove compartment. They were on good track to make it back home before nightfall, assuming that they only made one more stop.

Ted pulled off the highway, driving their little thunderbird into a gas station at the edge of a town. The two of them got out, car parked in the shade of a sycamore tree, Ted filling up the car while Mary-Beth stretched her legs.

"Lunch?" He asked, fishing his wallet out of the car. "We can walk into town."

Mary-Beth nodded, putting on her hat and fanning out her fringe. They wandered down the main street - it was a quiet day for a Saturday, the air warm, not many people on the street. There was a diner ten minutes away, an open sign hanging in the window. She had a rosary clutched between her fingers.

The inside was all polished beech wooden floors, shiny tables, paper menus. A bubbly, auburn-haired waitress led them to a red leather booth, her white blouse neatly pressed, silverware tucked into her lace lined apron. Mary-Beth gazed out the window while Ted perused the menu, rattling out his burger decisions and whether he should have a milkshake or a float.

The street outside was bright, fun colours, neat shop windows, well-kept roofs. Their waitress took their orders, bringing out Ted's bacon cheeseburger and her house salad quickly. Something felt off. Her water had a lemon slice without her having to ask, Ted's milkshake had an extra cherry. The waitress wished them a safe journey home. On their walk back through the town, Ted offered to step into shops, pick up flowers or chocolates or more magazines for the drive. Mary-Beth shook her head no, trying to subtly increase her pace. Her skin was crawling.

They made it back to the car without a hitch. Ted drove them down the main street, not a pothole in sight, and it took everything in Mary-Beth not to duck under the dashboard and pray. The rest of their trip was smooth, making it to their slightly quieter two-bedroom house - neat lane, white picket fence, leftovers in the fridge. Mary-Beth spoke to their daughter on the phone, watching Ted lock the front door. Double-checking it was locked before she followed him up to bed.

She couldn't shake the feeling of that town. It took her a few hours to fall asleep, tossing and turning while Ted snored beside her. The sleep she did get was confused, restless, ending in shakes and tremors.

It was the next morning, over her second cup of coffee and a pastry swallowed down as she waved Ted off for work, when she realised exactly what had bothered her so much about that town. Of all the towns they had driven past and through on their trip, it was the only one that was not cowering in the shadow of a church spire. The air didn't have space in it for a single prayer.

Chapter Three

When the 7.30am bell rang for the first class at Lovely High School the next morning, Heather was still in bed, sheets pulled up to her ears. Her dad had slammed the door on his way out, hard enough to shake her door frame and jolt her to consciousness. Sure, sweat was pooling under her knees, but she could hide in bed as long as she wanted-

"The front door was open so I let myself in."

She bolted up and Tyler was in her doorway, head touching the top of the frame, takeaway cup in hand. He was wearing a wrinkled navy shirt, and his hair hadn't been brushed. She wondered if anyone noticed when he left the house this morning.

"Coffee?" He handed her the cup. It had milk in it. Probably sugar too.

"Never fucking do this again."

"You're a delight in the morning," he sat down on the bed, almost sloshing the coffee onto her. "What's our plan?"

Heather took a sip, doing her absolute best not to panic. "*Our*? Ew." She tried to rub the sleep from her eyes. "Start at the lake, see if we find anything. Go upstream, ask around. Take it from there."

"Sounds good. Leaving in five?" He was smiling at her. It was too early for this.

"Sure," she set the cup down on her bedside table. "Let me change."

"Okay." He wasn't moving. She didn't think he'd ever been in her room before.

Heather changed with her back to him, as behind the closet door as she could physically be. Tyler was looking at the magazine cut-outs on her walls, the mess of her furniture, her cassette tape collection. She was almost being scrutinised. Hopefully he won't find the D- report cards and pregnancy tests.

"How did you get my address?"

"What do you mean?" He was trying too hard to be casual. He won't look at her.

"You've never been here before. How do you know where I live?" There were no shivers running down her spine. That makes it worse.

"I got your address from the school front desk. I have contacts there." He flashed her an easy smile. "Promise I'm not stalking you."

"Do you have any contacts in the sheriff's office?" She meant it more as a joke, but it's a flat delivery.

"No." He's serious, and she's ruined it. "Do you?"

"Only in like, a really bad way," Heather steps out from the closet, clad in loose jeans, a bulky sweater, her hair pulled up. "Ready?"

"Always." He's looking just past her.

A tensely quiet, twenty minute car ride later, Heather and Tyler are staring down the banks to the lake. There are green sycamore leaves leading down the loose dirt slopes, dipping into the murky depths of the water. The ground is trampled with footprints and scraps of police tape, in a way that reminds Heather this place was once beautiful. Now it's the track marks up to the road where Max Henderson's body was dragged by the hands of strangers.

Tyler's eyes are focused hard on a spot far ahead, somewhere between the trees. Heather pays it no mind - she's scanning the ground in front of her, looking for anything that could be considered a clue. The water is peaceful, and the lake is empty. It wouldn't be surprising if they were the only people down here today, or any other day. It may have been more surprising that Max's body was found in the first place.

> *The Lucky Times*
> *Figure one. All three members of the Spart family reunited.*
> *THE SPART FAMILY, after four gruelling days of their youngest daughter being a missing person, are finally back together. Max Spart reported his daughter, Bethany Spart, aged 5, missing on the 29th of August. After a county wide search, a strenuous community effort, and a thorough police investigation, Bethany was found on the banks of the town lake, in a soaked through school dress and barefoot. The family is grateful to have her back, and are not answering any questions at this time. MICK S.*

This is the third door they have knocked on in the same hour. The man who opens it is middle aged, tired looking, open beer in hand. He stands on a threadbare carpet dotted with faded stains.

Tyler launches into his spiel. "Hi, sorry to disturb you. We're young volunteers with the Sheriff's department and we were wondering if you heard or saw anything suspicious two nights ago? That's Sunday night." He's given the exact same speech twice before - two slammed doors. Heather's job here is to hold a pen and notepad, and look ready to jot down any details. Strictly speaking, she has no stake in the matter.

The man looks Tyler up and down, his easy going smile, his wrinkled shirt. Heather is selling their story less than he is. Another slammed door.

Forty minutes and twelve failed attempts later, the two of them are walking upstream, Heather's calves burning at the rocky uphill climb. Tyler hasn't said a word since the last house. They make it up to a patch of dirt where the ground flattens out, under a metal bridge that freight trains run over so fast it shakes the rails. Heather reaches up to brush some rust off the underside, fingers grabbing at a metal flake painted red- and her foot slips on loose packed dirt, crashing down. Tyler catches her, picking her up and close.

"Oh-"

"Sorry," he sets her back down, hands lingering on her back and elbow. She was airborne for just a single second, cradled. No big deal.

"Look." There's a scrap of fabric snagged on the bolts of the bridge, just above where Heather's pointing. Tyler pulls it down, one hand still on the small of her back. She's not moving away either. The fabric is starched cotton, cream coloured, a seam down the middle. No convenient nametag.

"It's a start," Heather tries weakly.

Tyler shrugs, tucks it into his back pocket. "We should head back. I can still make the fourth period."

"I can walk back," Heather trails behind him downhill, hands in her back pockets.

"Don't be ridiculous." He doesn't snap at her, but she wishes he would.

They're back in the car before she knows it, her feet on the dashboard, him fiddling with the radio. She wants to tell him to skip school, to go to her place, to buy them lunch. She tells him to turn that shit off instead.

Tyler slows his car on main street, about a half mile from her house. Heather reaches for her door handle, and then his mouth is on hers, one hand gripping the collar of her sweater. She pulls back, aware they're on a main road, aware he's looking at her like she has all the answers for him.

"Someone could see," she says, at the same time as he says, "Let me drive you home."

"What? No," Heather pulls back, trying to shrink herself against the seat. "It's daytime, and we're in public."

"And?" He's acting like he's not lying.

"And you're an asshole." She's acting like she can't hear him as she walks away.

About fifty years ago, Lovely started its first ever summer camp. It wasn't the most unexpected move - a couple of neighbouring towns full of bored teenagers and a lake that stayed tranquil and cool on the hottest of the days was a money making haven. A handful of wooden cabins were built on the slopes up from the lake, and a group of teachers and recent graduates recruited as camp counsellors, so the camp was ready to go. It was mostly watersports, building newer cabins, and basic woodland skills such as tent making and starting small fires.

Ten years later Camp Lovely was in full swing. July first, the school buses would roll in, full of ready campers for two months of hot summer until they were carted back to their town of origin. There were plans to expand to larger, busier cities further away, where parents with bigger pockets lived, and the next summer was going to be the biggest yet. Sadie, who had graduated the high school a few months earlier and wanted to get a little more work experience before she moved a state over to live with her cousin, was the newest camp counsellor on the team. Her mother took a photo of her in her freshly cleaned orange shirt on her first day and stuck it on the fridge.

Sadie loved the kids she worked with, and the feeling of being out on the lake. She could paddle her kayak to the middle and pretend she wasn't still stuck in the same town she had been born in, pretend the current was open water sweeping her away, to new shores. Her team was eager, enjoyed her lessons on forest safety and led the way on clearing back the trees for cabin number nine. The first weekend that Sadie had off she spent lying in a hammock strung up in her back garden, nursing a bottle of her dad's beer and wondering what was happening at camp.

She was there fifteen minutes early on Monday, the sun barely up, her little car crunching damp leaves. The other counsellors - a group of mostly teachers, some of which she had had last semester - had a mug of coffee ready for her, as well as a clipboard detailing extra responsibilities for her. She was more than happy to do morning checks on the five existing cabins, slightly happy to be off kitchen duty. The cabins were spread out in a circle around this side of the lake, each a ten minute walk from each other, well-lit by a combination of metal torches and the rising sun.

Sadie was there, clipboard in hand, smile at the ready. Her first cabin didn't answer when she knocked - understandably, given that it was only just seven a.m. and their second week here. She gave them the benefit of the doubt. By the third cabin that met her with silence, she was starting to worry. Sadie sped past cabin four to cabin five, her cabin, who she'd spent twelve hours a day with the past week, who she had started to get to know.

"Cabin Five? It's fifteen minutes past wake up, you should be ready. Cabin Five? If I don't hear a response, I am going to have to come in. Cabin Five, I need to hear something. I'm coming in."

The scene inside the cabin was bloody. The sun cast rays of light on the twelve campers, the red staining the floor, the messy handprints on the walls. Bodies still in their bunks, throats slit, crumpled piles of limbs on the floor where they tried to run. One closet door ripped off its hinges, the clothes inside scarlet-stained as the kid hiding in there was dragged out. His guts were spilled out as punishment.

Sadie took two trembling steps back outside the cabin, turning and vomiting into the closest bush. She staggered back down the path, forcing open the door to cabin four.

An equal mess. All twelve kids dead, one a crimson mess under the bunk bed, the window in the back of the cabin shattered. Blood in the cracked glass. Cabin three was just as bad, sheets pulled off the beds, curtains stained with bleeding fingerprints. The bodies in cabin two were beginning to rot in the sun, the stench of death hitting her before she could even open the door, as futile as it was. Cabin one had begun to attract flies, the buzz droning through Sadie's ears and muffling her cries for help. She was screaming at this point.

She staggered into the cabin reserved for camp counsellors, painted with cheery orange stripes and smelling like freshly brewed coffee. Sadie fell through the door, not knowing how her hands got covered in blood, death in her hair, eyes watering. The room was empty, beds stripped, full mugs left unattended. There was not a single other living person in the camp grounds. The lot was empty of cars, just the track marks in the dirt left behind.

When they found Sadie - curled up in a kayak in the middle of the lake, covered in blood, tears dried on her face - it was night. She hadn't come home. The sheriff's office ran out of body bags, the town morgue out of beds. Next week, the standing cabins were torn down and the wood burnt, including the camp signs and flyers posted on school notice boards. The lake was stripped of its brightly coloured ropes and lifeguard chairs, and the hammocks were dragged down and to the next town's dump.

Sadie, the last time anyone in Lovely had heard of her and before people couldn't bear to press her parents with any more questions, was in some kind of psychological hospital several hours upstate. That morning had broken her, had snapped something in her brain. She loved working with children. The last time she was seen, she was sitting on a cot in the centre of a cinderblock room, rocking back and forth in a paper gown. Sadie still woke up every morning ready to brave that lake with her cabin full of campers.

There were no arrests made for what happened in the cabins. The teachers had all either given false names on their applications, or driven far enough that they couldn't be reached anymore. One of the emergency contacts reached a bakery in New York. With no more leads or town members to pin the crowd on - Sadie now being out of bounds - the sheriff's office deemed it a cold case. The files, it was rumoured, found their way into a different burn pile. There was no summer camp in Lovely after that.

It took until two p.m. the next day for Tyler to call Heather back. She hadn't gone to school that day either, instead electing to spend the time curled up on the couch, hands around a chipped mug of hot tea. She was very intensely watching the sitcom playing on the television, and was not at all thinking of the casserole her father had, with no explanation, placed in the fridge last night. It was almost a relief when the phone rang.

"Hello-"

"It's me. I need your help."

"Tyler? I-"

"Please don't talk."

There was a moment of silence. Heather bit her lip.

"I need your help. I heard my parents talking last night. I think something's wrong."

His voice sounded weird, hoarse. Did he spend the whole night yelling?

"Can you meet me at the bridge? Ten minutes."

She tried not to breathe too hard into the speaker.

"Oh my god, you can talk now."

"See you in ten." She hung up before he could say anything.

When Heather rounded the bend to the bridge, Tyler was already there - liquor bottle in hand, car parked, leaning back on the railing. There was a weird dark stain on his denim jacket, and his stance seemed unsteady. This was going to be a hell of an afternoon.

"Tyler?" Her hands are tucked securely in her jean pockets.

His eyes looked to hers, and his lit up ever so faintly. "Heather!" He started stumbling over, needing to lean on the hood of his car. His hand reached for her.

"Hey, buddy," she stayed just out of reach. "You okay?"

"Nope," he shrugged, taking a strong, over-confident swing of his flask. "Drink?"

"Okay," she plucked it out of his hand, mostly to take it from him. A baby gulp. This is fine.

"Can I get you home? Are your parents out?"

"Don't know. What time is it?" He stared directly into the sun. Genius.

"When does your mum get home?" His dad had been staying at the only bar in town until close, she would guess by the fact that her father smelled like malt liquor every single time he staggered in, and the fact that the liquor store had stopped serving that pair five years ago.

"Her shift ends at five p.m.? I think. Thanks for coming today." His speech was getting more slurred by the second.

"Don't mention it. Give me your keys?"

"Okay!" He fumbled into his pocket, fishing out the keychain. There was a blue luggage tag on it with a badly drawn sailboat and his name in a child's scrawl drawn on the white paper insert.

Heather had to fasten him into the passenger seat, mostly because both of his hands were out of the window. She turned the radio to the traffic report, cranking her window down as they cruised down the mostly empty town streets.

They reached Tyler's house, his head resting on the window, eyes drooping shut. Heather parked his car in the drive, winding up her window. He stayed in the car.

"Tyler?"

"Mm-mm."

"Tyler, get out of the car."

"Don't wanna."

"Tyler, come on."

She had to haul him out of the car, sagging under his body, dragging him up the front porch steps. The key was under the flowerpot, the living room first door on the left, bottled water on the top shelf of the fridge - as it had been their whole childhood. Tyler was stretched out on the couch, shoes on the coffee table, head in his hands.

"Drink this," she forced the water bottle into his hand. "What's going on?"

He took a long, gulping drink, dribbling down his chin. Heather leaned against the wall, hands behind her back.

"Police were here last night. Talked to my parents. They're closing my brother's case. There isn't enough information. It's just over."

"It's not over-"

"Isn't it?" He's giving her that look again, the one that makes her feel like she's the one stopping him. It's fine. "The police stopped searching. I don't think there's anything more I can do."

"You'll figure it out." She was trying really hard not to look at any of the family photos on the mantelpiece. "There are still more people to talk to, and things the cops missed, and-"

"You'll help me?" Tyler reached out for her, his hands grasping. Her grip on the floral wallpaper tightened.

"Yeah. Of course I will."

※

If you stopped in Lovely to, let's say, ask for directions, you would be met with your standard small-town politeness. They would give you cardinal information, tell you when you'd know you had gone too far, and wish you a safe journey. Nothing more, nothing less. It would be the kind of occurrence that you would barely think about after you were safely home and your journey done, in a way that you couldn't pick out the town on the map the next day.

If you were out of fuel, however, that was a different story. It got to the frequency that the gas station employees a town over began noting down the descriptions of their patrons to look for on police-issued missing posters the next month. One couple, after their car was taken in for repairs and they booked a room in a local hotel, claims they were chased through woodland by a chainsaw-wielding mechanic until sunrise. A college student driving home for the summer stumbled, holding together what used to be his arm, into a twenty-four hour liquor store two towns over. An aspiring writer was found slumped over her steering wheel, passenger seat filled with empty liquor bottles, brake lines cut.

There were questions asked, of course. But it's easy to confuse which small town someone could have last been seen at - roads close, plans change, maps get lazy in rural areas. It's easy to forget an unfamiliar face when so many of them pass through your town, stopping in for food and fuel, only there for a few hours. It's not hard to hide a car when you have a bottomless lake and a dark forest at your disposal.

For a few years, people in the town over would warn locals to avoid Lovely. Gas station employees would advise you to fill your tank up all the way, just in case, and to bring some extra food for the road. But people forget, and employees leave for brighter futures, and the warnings stop. The deaths became less common, more of a strange occurrence than the terror-fuelled legend they once were. Not to say that they stopped.

It was noon the next day, and Heather was watching dust swirl through the air in front of a filing cabinet in the sheriff's office. She was slumped on an obviously cheap metal chair, jacket sleeves pulled over her hands, in front of an empty desk. The deputy she spoke to on the way in had told her she would be seen in five minutes - the clock on the wall said it had been twenty. She wondered if anyone would come check if she slammed her head on the wooden desk before her.

"He's ready for you." The deputy was younger than she remembered, his sleeves rolled over his elbows. There were shadows under his eyes and a coffee stain next to the holster on his waist. Her eyes lingered.

"Thanks." She straightened up, hard, making sure her feet didn't drag as she pushed open the door. The beige, slightly stained blinds rustled as she did so, cracking wood clacking to announce her presence. A legal beaded curtain.

The office was small, cramped, the tile floors a little sticky and the walls in need of a new coat of paint. Clearly whatever budget allocated to a small town sheriff's department was not being spent on the interior of the building. The back wall was lined with loose sheets of paper falling behind the metal radiator and getting themselves pinned under the desk. There was a yellowed, dead plant in a cement planter next to the door.

"Heather," the sheriff was sat at his desk, shirt pressed and spotless, mug of coffee still letting off steam. "Take a seat."

The small wooden chair in front of her scraped the floor and wobbled the second she sat down. It was lower than the desk - probably intentionally - and forced her to look up at the sheriff. He enjoyed that.

"It's been a while since I've seen you," the sheriff smiled, the gesture not quite reaching his blue eyes. "How have you been?"

"Good." She'd answered too fast. "All things considered."

He nodded, in a way that seemed like he was feigning wisdom. "I'm glad to hear. What brings you in today?"

Heather's hands curled, nails biting into her palms. "My, um -"

Tyler wouldn't exactly be happy if the sheriff knew about their friendship.

"My father's friend, Mr Henderson, lost his youngest son recently and he's really broken up about it and I-"

There was a layer of scepticism on the sheriff's face. Heather wished she could fake cry.

"My dad's really broken up about it, and he's worried about me, and I wanted to ask if there was anything that might reassure him? I mean, drained of blood is horrible, and who would do that to a kid, and I just-"

"I understand." The sheriff leaned back in his chair, hands folded over his stomach. He took a long pause, as if this was an interrogation and he was hoping she would confess if he made the tension in the room strong enough.

"Obviously, the investigation is closed. There are no further leads, and there is no more information we can give the family."

His voice was rigid, formal. Then he leaned forward, resting his elbows on the desk, fingers steepled. Heather waited for the other shoe to drop.

"But, I can say that this was not a murder. Whatever happened to Matt wasn't done by a human hand. We've handed the case over to the state, who have the park rangers and the money and the resources to investigate that simply aren't at my disposal. Once they establish a cause of death, we'll notify the family."

Heather nodded. That was a perfectly plausible explanation that made sense and she had no reason to doubt.

The sheriff flipped open a file on his desk. "Thank you for stopping by, Heather. I wish there was more I could do to help."

"Thank you," Heather forced herself out of the chair, seeing herself out of his office and letting the door swing shut behind her.

"Don't be a stranger," the detective called after her as she left the station, her cheeks grateful to be in the afternoon light. She took a hurried turn left, heading down the narrow alley that took her to main street - she crossed the almost empty road, taking the next alley that spit her out to the woods. And then she was running, through trees and uphill until she reached the top of the bank, skidding down the slope, lungs on fire, eyesight blurring. The sheriff had given her a perfectly reasonable explanation that she had no reason to question or doubt.

Except for the fact that he'd gotten Max Henderson's name wrong.

Travis Windsor, as anyone would tell you, was not a paranoid man. He worked a very respectable job in a bank the next town over, where he spent most of his time denying loans and approving withdrawals of large cash sums. Every morning, he would wake up just before dawn, kiss his still-sleeping wife goodbye, and drive his expensive, but not flashy, car down Main Street. He would stop at the diner, one of the few patrons and the only one in a suit and tie, for coffee, eggs, and the morning paper, before beginning his half hour drive. Travis would take his lunch at one, at the sandwich shop he could see from his desk, and finish work at five. He would be home for six p.m. dinner, where his two sons - twelve and nine - told him about their day at school, and he would go to bed shortly after the eleven o'clock news and three glasses of Scotch. This had been his routine for the past twenty years.

That Wednesday morning in September was no different. He rose, shaved in the bathroom mirror, kissed his wife goodbye. Travis's car cruised through the suburbs, coming to a stop in the parking lot just behind the diner. He stepped out of the car, briefcase in hand, and rounded the pavement to the diner door fifty feet away. As he often did, he noted how inconvenient it was to place the only door so far from the nearest parking spot.

There was another man walking down the otherwise empty street towards him. He also wore a neat black suit and a charcoal grey tie, his hands in his pockets. He appeared freshly shaven, his brown hair slicked back. He held Travis' gaze as the two passed each other, without offering any kind of greeting. He actually looked exactly like Travis.

Travis thought nothing of it. He pushed the glass door open, casting a final glance down the street. It was deserted.

The diner had its usual early morning crowd. There was the construction worker, already in a stained shirt and overalls, digging into a pancakes and eggs breakfast that seemed to grow bigger each month, washed down with several glasses of soda. The teacher who always looked more haggard, wrapped in a shawl and pinstriped blazer, stirring sugar into a hot tea. A grocery store clerk who looked far too stressed for his job description, binder open on the table next to his bacon platter, scribbling a tiny font with a cracked ink pen.

Bernie - his favourite member of the morning shift - was there, on the other side of the counter to his usual seat. A cup of coffee, creamer, and sugar, was sat next to a copy of this morning's paper. Bernie smiled at him, looking up through an auburn fringe and a light purple eyeshadow.

"Morning. How do you want your eggs today, sir?"

Bernie was his favourite member of the morning shift because she remembered his coffee order, and looked pretty in the grey shirt and yellow apron that was her uniform. If he asked her any more questions, he would learn that she had recently turned seventeen and had a boyfriend of three years who was the star of the track team - but Travis was more interested in someone who would get him the morning paper for a four dollar tip.

"Scrambled, please," he forced a smile, sliding into his seat.

"Extra pepper, buttered toast?" Bernie didn't have a notepad in hand. At this point, the line cooks knew his order.

"You got it, sweetheart," Travis flashed her a smile, eyes already scanning the newspaper.

Fifteen minutes later, coffee drained and plate cleared, Travis was getting back into his car. He sped out of Lovely, ready for his day at work. He checked his rear view mirror while at the crossroads before leaving the town limits. The stranger he had passed on his way the diner was stood on the pavement, staring straight at him. His doppelganger.

Travis threw himself into his work that morning. He scoured applications, studied backgrounds, double checked paperwork for the first time. If he hadn't been reminded about lunch by one of his coworkers, he may have forgotten.

At one o' three he was at the sandwich shop, his usual, ready to place his order. He didn't feel his usual Monte Cristo, instead deciding to opt for a Reuben. His cashier was a freckled twenty-something, who asked for his name three times before he registered it fully.

"Oh, Travis W.? We have your order ready?" He scurried over to the 'ready' counter, presenting a paper wrapped sandwich. It was a Reuben.

Travis bit into it at his desk, enjoying the medley of flavours on his tongue, refusing to think about the mystery behind the order. The sandwich shop seemed to have gotten new windowsill plants, in a way that he enjoyed. Travis glanced down at his calendar, which placed his schedule at less than busy for the rest of the afternoon. Lucky, he would have thought usually. Not today.

Travis slugged through his next few hours, head down, trying to focus far too hard on his work. His shift ended what felt like centuries after his lunch. He bid the boss's assistant - young, blonde, beaming, no further questions asked - goodbye, sliding into his car and speeding to the nearest highway, trying to make it home before anything else unsettling can happen, no matter how small.

The streets of Lovely were mostly empty, other than the few individuals he usually saw on his way home. He slowed down as he passed the diner, telling himself it was in case of pedestrians - but he was craning his neck to peer inside, just in case. The man in the suit - the man that looked like him - was sat there, perfectly still, staring straight ahead. Travis drove home, trying desperately to shake off his unease, his palms leaving sweaty trails on the steering wheel.

His house was warm, a refuge, yellow lights shining out into the growing dusk. He locked the front door behind him, making sure to slide the deadbolt into place, trying the handle before he set down his keys.

"Welcome home, honey!" His wife called from the kitchen. He could smell the meatloaf in the oven, watch her sautéing onions, roasted potatoes already served onto plates - his favourite. She beamed at him through the doorway, her honey curls shining, a powder blue apron tied around her waist. A glass of scotch sat ready for him on the counter.

"Hi sweetheart," he kissed her, hand already curling around the glass. Through the archway into the living room he could see their sons, eyes glued to the television screen, a half-eaten plate of chocolate chip cookies in front of them.

"How was work?" His wife asked, hands smoothing down his shirt collar.

"Not bad. How was school for the boys?"

"Good. Petey did well on his spelling test."

"That's my boy." Travis took a hearty swig of scotch. He was home now, and everything was fine.

"Can you take the trash out before dinner, please?" His wife had turned back to the stove, turning off the heat on the onions. He tried to remember if she was smiling or not.

"Sure." He finished his drink, lifting the plastic bag that was slumped against the back garden door. Travis stepped outside, the night already dark but illuminated by the warm lights of the house behind him. He crossed the stone pathway through his lawn, next to the flowerbeds his wife tended to, and unlatched the fence to the small alley at the very back. A single streetlight fifteen feet away lit up the dumpster which his wife was too anxious to visit after sundown, for some reason.

Travis lifted the lid and dropped the bag in, his mind already turned to the meatloaf his wife would have been plating right now. He wondered if dessert would be the lemon pie she had bought the ingredients for a few days ago, or if that was being saved for the weekend. He turned, ready to head home.

There was a figure stood in front of his garden gate, at the very edge of the circle of light cast by the streetlight. He could see polished leather shoes, a pressed dark suit, a white shirt and a grey tie. If it wasn't a ridiculous coincidence, he would say it was the exact same outfit he was wearing.

"Good evening," he said, taking a step forward. "I didn't see you when I first came down."

The figure was silent, still. Its hands were tucked into its pockets.

"My name is Travis. I live right up here - I guess I'm not as active in the neighbourhood as I would like to be."

The figure took a single, purposeful stride forward, straight into the streetlight's perimeter. Its well pressed white collar and sharp suit sat comfortably on its shoulders, where what looked like a wolf mask was on his head. The grey, tangled fur was surprisingly high quality and realistic - the bright yellow eyes felt like they were staring right at him, and it even looked like there was a string of drool trailing from its red lips.

Travis almost laughed. "Bit early for Halloween, don't you think?"

The figure took a step closer. They were exactly the same height, Travis noted distantly.

"I do admire your commitment, though. Don't let my sons see - they'll be wanting my missus to make them something just as good!"

"Oh, don't worry," the figure spoke, and it sounded like Travis' voice exactly, mimicking back at him. The mouth and lips moved as if it wasn't a mask, as if it was actual muscle and skin. "I'll make sure they don't see a thing."

The polite half-smile didn't have a chance to slide from Travis' face when the creature lunged at him, hands pulling out of its pockets to reveal clawed wolf paws. Its yellow teeth sunk into his throat, tearing out the muscles of his windpipe while its paws dug out his still beating heart, his blood glinting black in the moonlight. Travis tried to scream - instead he could only watch as the figure crawled onto his chest, its now scarlet soaked muzzle inches away from his face, the pearly white of his own ribs winking up at him.

"I need to see what your face looks like," his own voice said, coming from the lips of the thing, its claws digging deeper into his chest. "One last time."

Its teeth ripped through his heart next, blood drenching Travis' shirt as it chewed through the muscle, swallowed. It bit at his chest, stripping off pieces of skin, gulping them down. It flipped his body over like it was nothing, pulling up his suit and shredding off a piece of his white shirt. The thing raised the shirt up to its face, wiping off the blood and drool - and when it lowered it, it wore Travis' face, had Travis' hands, down to the calluses on his palms he got from working his uncle's farm in the summers when he was a teenager. It pulled his wedding ring and his watch off of Travis' body, attached them to its own hand, and dropped the corpse into the dumpster, careful to position a couple of bags of trash on top. It walked up the path, stepping inside Travis' garden and making sure to latch the gate behind it. You never know what could be lurking out there in the dark, after all.

It walked into Travis' kitchen, where his wife had just finished placing dinner on the table and had poured him a second glass of scotch.

"Thank you for doing that," she beamed, reaching up to wipe a drop of sweat off of his cheek.

"Of course, darling. Anything for you," the thing smiled, following her and taking a seat at the head of the table. "Thank you for making my favourite."

She smiled back, the sons already sat around the table. It reached over and brushed a strand of hair out of its youngest's eyes - gentle, paternal.

"How was school?" It asked, slicing off a bite of meatloaf, taking another sip of the scotch. Nothing out of place, just a normal dinner with Travis' family. With its family.

Chapter Four

HEATHER CALLED TYLER FROM THE PHONE inside the liquor store a half mile from her house, the same one where she used to buy beer for her dad when she was twelve. The cashier was a few years older than her, dark hair in her eyes, flipping through a magazine while chewing gum, her lips painted a bright red. She'd probably gone to the only high school in town, frequented the same diner, gotten drunk in the same alleys and woodland copses. Maybe she was the cheer team captain, certain she'd leave this town behind and make it in the big city only to find her feet had always been stuck in the tar. Maybe she always knew she would die in her hometown.

The phone picked up on the fourth ring.

"Tyler? I need you to come pick me up, I-"

"Who is this?"

It's Tyler's father on the phone. The last time she saw Mr Henderson must have been almost seven years ago, back when she was still invited to birthday parties and ate cake. She remembered him being late, dressed in a black suit and tie, briefcase clenched in his hand the whole time.

"Sorry, sir," her brain was scrambling to remember any of Tyler's friends. "My name is Bethany. I'm one of Tyler's friends, and he told me to call him. I'm just worried."

"I don't think my son would want to talk to you." Mr Henderson said slowly.

"Can you please just ask? If he says no, I won't bother you again."

Mr Henderson sighed down the line. The cashier gave Heather an irritated look, then opened a new magazine.

"I'll ask."

Heather tried to stop the smile flashing across her face. She heard Mr Henderson, muffled, yelling that Bethany was on the line. An even quieter response.

"He'll take the call in his room. Don't be on the line too long."

"Yes sir," Heather forced out, tapping her foot because she couldn't pace. There was a second of silence.

"Bethany doesn't have this number." Tyler. Thank fuck.

"I know, it's me. Sorry I lied to your dad."

"Don't be. Why are you calling?"

"I have something to tell you. Can you come pick me up?"

"Sure. Where are you?"

"You know the liquor store off main street?"

"Okay, I'll be there in ten."

"Tyler."

"What?"

"Don't tell anyone where you're going."

"Okay, weirdo." He hung up.

When Tyler was eight years old, he saw something scary. Not a movie or a late night television program or a ghost story - something real, and something bad. It was the kind of scary that cemented itself in his memory as a terrifying thing, that still woke him up at night all these years later, that blurred out all the negatives that happened before it. He had forgotten the hours as a child he spent listening to his parents scream at each other, or the time he broke his arm on the playground and still had to walk home alone, or the comments his uncle made at his first baseball game. It was the kind of bad that drowned everything else out.

He was eight years old, and his little brother Max had just turned two. Tyler had two main objectives - he had to dry the dishes after dinner, and he had to make it home safely after school. His class would end at three, and it would be five p.m. before his mother and Max made it home. Home was only a fifteen minute walk from the school, and he wore his key around his neck in a cold weight all day. Sometimes some of his friends would walk part way with him, sometimes he would sprint home and make the most of choosing what he could watch on the television and raiding the snack cabinet. It usually went smoothly - his parents trusted him for a reason, and all he had to do was wait patiently until his mother got home.

One day, the same as any other, Tyler made his own way home. His friend Ben and Ben's mother walked most of the way with him - they lived a couple of streets over, and him and Ben had class together - and after that it was a straight shot to his house, the door locked behind him, television on and half a container of store-bought brownies with his name on it.

About twenty minutes into an after school special, Tyler heard what sounded like a faint scratching from the back door. He didn't think anything of it - it was probably a tree branch in the wind, or someone else's cat begging to be let in. A laugh track rang out from the television.

The scratching got louder, faster. Tyler sat up straighter on the couch, suddenly very aware that he was alone in the house and likely would be for the next hour. The scratching was probably nothing. He didn't know what he was supposed to do if it was something.

The television was on mute now, his eyes barely glancing at the screen. He couldn't ignore the scratching any longer. His instincts told him to stay where he was, to be quiet and hope it went away - but he needed to be an adult about this. He was in charge of the house when his parents weren't there. It was his duty to see what all the noise was about.

He reached the kitchen, padding over wooden floorboards as quietly as he could. The back door loomed before him, impossibly tall in the face of his grass-stained school shirt. *Just a cat*, he told himself, forcing his hand to latch onto the door handle. Tyler swallowed hard, jerking the back door open.

The scratching was not a cat, or a tree branch. Instead, kneeling at the door, reaching shoulder height for him was a man, chest bare, trousers shredded. He had the salt and pepper hair of Tyler's father, his finger was a battered, bloody mess from scraping at the wood panel. The man looked up and it was Max's face, stretched thin over adult bones and blown into uncanny proportions, mouth hanging open laxly as if he hadn't gotten the hang of jaws yet.

Tyler screamed, slamming the door shut and drawing the bolt over it. He scrambled to the kitchen, wrenching a knife from the drawer and making it up the stairs. There he sat, back against the wall of his room, knife trained on the door, holding his breath as he waited for the scratching to start up again. It never did.

Instead, his mother came home at five past five. Max begged him to watch cartoons and, although it was a little hard to look him in the eyes, Tyler obliged. His father painted over the deep scrapes on the back door that weekend, and the damage was blamed on raccoons.

All these years later, Tyler still wakes up in the night, throat hoarse from screaming, hands grasping at the switchblade he keeps on his bedside table. When his father broke down in the town morgue and couldn't bear to look at his brother's water bloated corpse, he felt a small flicker of hope that maybe, the ballooned and deformed image he saw at night would be his brother's face - some strange, hellish premonition of the future. It wasn't.

The night that Heather came back into town, Tyler saw that face every single time he closed his eyes. A child's memory he couldn't quite shake.

Heather made him drive ten minutes out of town, pull into a dried-up ditch and lock the car doors before she said anything to him. Tyler wasn't exactly surprised - this used to be their old routine and, while he was a little irritated at the apparent step back, he was prepared for setbacks, prepared for anything when it came to her.

"Do you want me to pile old leaves onto the car before you start talking?" He joked, reclining his seat. Heather tried very hard not to glare at him.

"It's going to sound crazy," she shifted in her seat, crossing her legs and leaning back against the window. "But I went by the sheriff's office this morning and something seemed weird."

"Weird how?"

"Weird like he got your brother's name wrong," she blurted out. "Like he did not seem concerned, at all. He told me it wasn't done by a person, but what animal does this? What animal drains the blood of a kid but leaves the flesh alone, I mean if it was hungry wouldn't it-"

"I'm not a wildlife expert," Tyler snapped. He was staring straight ahead, at the forest all around them. "If he said it was an animal, it's an animal."

"But don't you think it's weird?" Heather's voice was gentler, more timid. She hated it. She was trying not to pry. "He didn't even name an animal. I thought he would offer an explanation-"

"That's not the sheriff's job."

"I would argue it is-"

"That's not for you to decide!" Tyler was yelling now, his hands gripping the steering wheel so hard his knuckles were burning white. "It's not *your* brother! You're just curious about this, you're involved for kicks-"

"That's not why-" Heather's voice was barely audible.

"What the fuck is your connection with the sheriff anyway?" Tyler had turned back to her, glaring her down. She shrunk back against the car door, the handle on her spine a familiar feeling. "What were you doing there?"

"I went to get answers," she forced out. "The sheriff's a family friend-"

"Shut *up*."

Tyler's fist cracked against the steering wheel, and she did. Heather took stifled, shallow breaths, nails biting into her palms, watching Tyler heave in air. A tense minute passed before he jabbed on the radio, car wheels spitting dirt as they moved back onto the road. They hurtled back to Lovely, Heather watching the speedometer creep up to seventy. She resisted the urge to grip the seat cushion.

They were coming up to a hairpin bend. "Tyler, the road."

"I know!" He slammed on the brakes, the car screeching to a halt. The seatbelt bit into Heather's chest, her hands flat on the dashboard. She waited until the leather strap loosened - and then she unclicked the seatbelt, shoved the door open and spilled out onto the road. Her legs felt like jelly but she kept moving, stumbling into the grassy bank and the bushes. She doubled over, throwing up coffee and whiskey and cheap soda. A hacking cough ripped through her throat, making her more desperate for comfort. She spat up bile and water, her mouth numbing.

"Hey."

She straightened up, fast, twisting around. The car's engine was off, Tyler leaning against the hood, his hands in his back pockets forcing nonchalance. Heather fought the urge to run.

"Car sick?"

She nodded. Tyler circled the car, a hawk among rabbits, cracking open the boot and pulling out a bottle of water and a can of beer. He walked over to her and she grabbed the beer.

He waited until she had gulped down half of it, looking just past her into the woods. "Look, I didn't mean it."

She sighed, almost too small to notice. "I know."

"I just-"

"I know."

He actually looked at her then. There were none of the usual signs she was upset, but he could see her clenched fist.

"I was ten when my mum died. I remember what it felt like." Her voice didn't waver and her gaze stayed steady. He wondered if the pit in his stomach was hers.

"I'm sorry," he ventured.

"Shut up," Heather drained the rest of the beer, shoving the empty can into his hands. She stomped back over to the car, right thumb rubbing over her open palm.

Tyler allowed himself a sliver of a smile. Sometimes, when it was a nice day out and his guard was down, he liked to imagine they could have been high school friends, if things were different.

"Hey," Heather called. Tyler looked up; the door to the car's backseat was open, and she was leaning back, one hand already undoing her belt.

"Jesus Christ." Tyler murmured, dropping the empty can and water bottle and trying not to sprint over. He actually smiled this time, pulling his shirt off and tossing it into the passenger seat.

Neither of them noticed the deer, camouflage in the shrubbery, watching them with blue eyes, its head cocked to one side - as a dog would.

At eight the next morning, while Heather was still fast asleep next to a paperback horror book, Tyler was getting ready for work. On weekends, he worked at the auto shop on main street until the early afternoon, the one between the florist and the newsagent's. It was a relatively easy job, mostly sweeping and stocking, with the occasional customer, and it made him enough money to put gas in his car and buy the occasional six pack. Plus, it got him out of the house on the few mornings his father might be there.

Tyler finished shaving in the sink, turning off the light and creeping back down the hallway. He changed into his work shirt and jeans, opening his blinds and making his bed. On his way downstairs, he paused at Max's room for a second, expecting to see him bundled up in the light green sheets, the stuffed rabbit his parents said he was too old for held in his arms. The bed was empty, the sheets still pulled back from where the police had rifled through. His chest twinged. The toy rabbit lay face down on the floor.

Tyler started his car, heavy work boots leaving sawdust on the passenger seat. He picked up coffee from a gas station on his way there, parking behind the store. His boss had first given him a key temporarily a few years back - now he used it to open the store alone on weekends. Shifts during the summer were harder; he would take on more hours, late nights, actual mechanic workloads, and try to act confident when his classmates drove in shiny cars and tossed him the keys. But it was still spring, and he watched the sunlight stream in as he rolled up the metal shutters of the store.

The next few hours sped by, quiet, and his boss was only five minutes late. Mr Kellan was the kind of man who carried himself with an air of importance and irreplaceability, despite his habit of confidently giving locals incorrect directions.

"Got a job for you, boy," he barked, his eyes looking anywhere but Tyler. This kind of off the clock errand was a regular occurrence - once, Tyler had to drive five hours to demand an oil change stock-up that had been delivered to the store a week earlier. It was the last thing he needed right now.

"There's a storage place out of town, in my aunt's name, and one of the rentals in it has a bunch of jacks. Head up and bring some down here." A key was dropped into the counter, and the door to the back swung shut. It took a moment for Tyler to realise the conversation was over.

He used the phone outside the diner to call Heather, the key burning a hole in his jacket pocket.

"Hello?"

"Did I wake you?" It was past two p.m. He still felt he had to ask.

"No, you didn't. What's up?"

"I have to drive an hour to this storage unit to check on something. Do you want to come with me? I'll buy you lunch."

He could hear the bristle in her voice. "I didn't think you would want to see me today."

Tyler turned away from the street, resting his head on the brick wall. "Well, I do."

"I can meet you on Main Street in ten?"

"Nice. I can pick you up, I think that would be easier-"

He heard Heather laugh, and then the line went dead.

Twenty minutes later, he watched Heather cross the road from where he was leaning on the hood of his car. She was wearing the oversized grey sweater he liked, as well as her usual jeans and leather boots. Her hair was held in a loose bun, her hands shoved deep in her pockets, a backpack strap over one shoulder. She didn't look at him until the car door shut behind her.

"Thank you for coming," he said, the engine purring.

"It's not like I had anything better to do," Heather shrugged, her feet up on the dashboard.

"Still." They sat in an uneasy silence as they left Lovely, winding down backroads and half-forgotten highways. The radio played a pop hit neither of them sang along to. Heather stared out of the window, playing with the lighter in her hands in a way that screamed fire hazard. Tyler didn't regret inviting her for a second.

"How was your night?" He asked, stealing a glance at her.

"The usual. Who's storage unit are we checking?"

"Uh, just a small favour my boss asked. Something to do with replacing jacks."

"You're giving out favours for free now?" Heather grinned, for the first time that morning, and it didn't matter that she was making fun of him. "What's next, you're running after school clubs?"

"I would do a better job than Mr Smith is now," he joked, and watched the smile slip off her face. The last time they had his class together, she had refused to meet his gaze and he'd spent the whole lesson flirting with Annie, who had just joined the cheerleading team. "Anyway, it's mostly just an out of hours task. Part of the job, you know."

Heather was trying not to visibly scoff at him.

"Again, thank you for coming along."

"I needed to get out of the house." Her eyes were back on the road, one hand picking at her lips.

"Have you tried coming to school?"

She actually scoffed at him that time. "What's the point? I have to repeat the year anyway."

"Wait," he fought to not look at her. "They're making you repeat the year? We won't have class together anymore."

"Lucky you," she said bitterly. "No one's said anything yet, not officially, but I'm about three months behind with a month left to make it up. It's not like I was ever the greatest student."

"I could help you study," Tyler offered, pulling onto the highway. "You could talk to some teachers, get your grades up a little with some extra work-"

"I don't think there's any point. None of our teachers like me that much."

"But-"

"Thanks anyway," Heather shrugged, pulling open her bag. "Gum?"

"What? No," Tyler watched her put three pieces in her mouth. "I just don't think you should give up on school when there's still a month left and-"

"Is this our exit?"

Heather was right. They pulled off the highway, parking in front of an overgrown brick building with metal shutters. There was a narrow wrought iron staircase up to the second floor, muddled with leaves and tiles loosened from the roof. The building looked deserted, crushed cans littering the lot, the wooden sign in front chipped and faded.

"Number six," Tyler strolled up to the door, unlocking it and pushing up the metal. It screeched like a strangled cat.

"Holy fuck."

The inside of the storage unit was papered with files, red wires, newspaper clippings, scribbled drawings. It spread to the floor and the ceiling, a tangled nest like a rat king. The papers were taped, pinned, scratched on with black ink. Faded photos of an all too familiar office, etchings of faces spiralling. The words *don't let them take me* scrawled in red lipstick by the threshold.

"What is this?" Heather asked, stepping onto the covered floor. The ceiling above her was a mess of missing posters and crime scene photographs.

"It doesn't look like an auto shop," Tyler pulled a ripped piece of blotter paper off the wall. *He's going to steal my face*, was written in looping handwriting. He passed it to Heather.

"What happened here?" She was looking at photos of missing children that had turned up dead, each one drained of blood.

"I don't know." Tyler picked up a flyer for something called Camp Lovely. "I just know it was his aunt's."

"You think she went mad?" She untacked a photocopy of what looked like a book on local folklore. Sections of it were highlighted, small notes inked in the margins.

"Seems like it," he picked up a picture of the sheriff, the words *it's him* inked on the back. "Do you think any of this actually means anything?"

"You know my thoughts on the sheriff," she snapped, grabbing the photo from him. Tyler didn't get offended, as a matter of fact. He was mostly happy she was talking to him.

"What if you're right?" He asked quietly, holding a newspaper clipping of a teenager found with his guts ripped out.

"What did you say?" She had heard him perfectly. She wanted him to say it again.

"Nothing. We should head back. Before it gets dark."

Heather shrugged, beginning to load up documents into her backpack. It would have taken a moving van to bring it all back with them. Tyler gave the unit a sweeping gaze, hoping a jack would jump out at him, before realising he actually didn't care that much.

Tyler rolled the metal door down, locking it and turning back to the car. If either of them had been inside when the door closed, they would have seen the red paint on the inside that spelled out *MIMICS*.

Chapter Five

Five years ago. Heather, drowning in her jeans and sweater, snug boots biting up the dirt hills behind their house. Her father was leading the way, marching for fifty minutes before he turned back. She was two steps behind him, shotgun in hand, wide eyes staring up at him. His mouth stayed a stoic line.

"You got a good handle on it?" He asked, stepping up five beer cans on the flat side of a three-foot rock. "Do you have it under control?"

"Yeah," Heather nodded. "Yeah, of course."

"Alright, kid," he took a few dozen steps back, moving until his back felt a tree trunk. "Take your best shot."

Heather took a deep breath, the weapon weighing down her arms, a pain already blossoming in her back. She grounded her feet, squared her shoulders, dragged the butt of the shotgun up to her shoulders. Pictured her father's face on one of the aluminium labels. Fired.

Heather fired five shots. Every single one pierced clean through the middle of a can. The sixth of the barrel hit the tree an inch above her father's head. He smiled.

"Good shots, kid." He walked over the dead leaves, pulled the gun from her blistered hands. "Moving targets next." He reloaded for her, forcing the trigger back into her arms.

"Dad?"

He didn't turn around, didn't even acknowledge her voice.

"Dad, why are we doing this again?"

"You need to be ready," he growled, throwing a can in a high and fast arc through the air.

"For what?" she asked, her voice drowned out by the firing sound of a gun.

It was the next day, and the two of them were sat in a diner thirty minutes out of town. There was a tray of fries on chequered paper in between them, a half drank vanilla milkshake, an empty glass of water. Tyler was biting into a cheeseburger, watching Heather pretend to reread the menu.

"Have a fry."

"What do you think any of the stuff we found means?" Heather asked, the menu dropped. The only other people in this diner, so big that it never looked busy, were a bored waitress and a truck driver digging into a piece of meatloaf. This was their usual spot for the rare occasions Tyler insisted they had a meal together - far enough out of town that they didn't run into anyone they knew, no liquor to entice either of their fathers, empty enough that they weren't bothered.

"Other than Mr Kellan's aunt went mad?" Tyler set down his burger, clear scepticism on his face.

"I mean, the storage unit definitely looked crazy." The slice of tomato he had discarded earlier was winking at her. "But those articles were real. The missing posters, the camp, the folktales, they're all things that happened. What if they are related?"

"The only thing they have in common is that they all happened in Lovely. You think that means something?"

"Maybe," Heather's stomach growled. "It's a weird coincidence, either way."

"Yeah, I guess," Tyler slid his milkshake over to her. "It's not like they're out of the ordinary."

"How about the fact that no one's ever heard of any of this? Like it's been covered up? I mean, I'd never heard of Lovely's summer camp, or any of those missing kids."

"I don't think that's that weird. No one really talks about bad news around here." He pushed the milkshake closer, more insistent. "When was the last time you heard anyone say anything about my brother, huh? And that was last week."

Heather nodded, ducking his gaze. She took a sip of the vanilla shake, cold and smooth and sweet. "Yeah, you're right."

"I know," he flashed her a smile, sadness in his eyes. "I can order you another burger, if you want."

She shook her head. "I did find something else, though."

"What?" He was back to the burger.

"So, whenever a crime is investigated in Lovely, there's a report made. Just basic information - what happened, who was involved, if any arrests were made or charges pressed." Heather sifted through the papers in her bag, half expecting to find her own police report. "It's a routine procedure, but the sheriff has to sign off on it, to verify that everything was reported correctly and no information is missing, right?"
"Where are you going with this?" Tyler watched her layer the photocopies of the reports on the diner table.

"This is a report from 1941, when Lucy Miller was the archivist. See the sheriff's signature?"

It was a breaking and entering case, concluding with the arrest of the neighbour's son. A gunshot was fired, but no one hurt. The sheriff's signature was a capital *S*, a scribbled star like a badge, and a looping scroll after it.

"Yeah."

"This is a report from 1890. Same signature." A bag of flour stolen from a store, in broad daylight. A father was arrested.

"So he was sheriff for a long time."

"This is from 1750, one of the first documents from Lovely. A land dispute. Same signature."

"Okay, so it's a family thing? The sheriff's office is a part of the inheritance?"

"This is from a month ago. Same signature."

Tyler looked down at the report, then up at her. "That's weird."

"Exactly. The name is exactly the same as well." She pulled a faded photograph out of her backpack. "This is a photo from 1851, when the high school first opened."

"Holy shit. That's the sheriff." He was there, dead centre, grinning at the camera. Wide brimmed hat, badge gleaming.

"Yeah. So either this is a very elaborate joke with no payoff-"

"Or the sheriff is over two hundred years old."

Heather hadn't wanted to say it out loud. But Tyler did, mouth slack, fingers gripping the table.

"You kids want anything else?"

She jumped, hard. The waitress had wandered over to them, refilling Heather's water, ice clinking too loud into the glass. It felt like there were bugs under her skin.

"Another milkshake?" Tyler asked, smooth, calm. Steady.

"Vanilla again? Coming up." She walked away, as Heather began packing the evidence back into her backpack.

The two of them sat in silence as she walked away. Tyler finally reached over, grabbing her hand, hard.

"People don't live to two hundred years old," he said slowly, as if he was speaking to a child. *Or someone who was losing it.*

"I know," she was trying very hard not to snap at him. *He always fucking disagrees with me.* "So what's your explanation?"

"I don't know. We should go to the library, or something. Get help."

"Not the-"

"No one can know about this." The waitress slid another milkshake onto the table, as well as the bill. They waited until she left.

"I know."

"I'm serious."

"Tyler," she did snap a little that time. Only a bit. "Who would I tell?"

The purposefully loud slurp of a milkshake through a straw was his only response.

It was a bright, summer day when the photo of the sheriff was taken. Lovely had just made the year's edition of *Top 100 Towns to Travel Through*, on account of its peaceful countryside, twenty-four hour diner, and low crime rate, and a big city photographer was coming into town to take a snapshot for the brochure. The whole town - all 156 residents - were abuzz.

There was a large, drawn out town debate, hosted in a mostly vacant Main Street, about where the photo should be taken and who should be in it. A vote for a picture of the lake, showcasing the picturesque nature of the town, almost won, as did the push for a picture of the new school; but the winning vote was to highlight the sheriff's department, responsible for keeping the town safe - not that it was hard to police a quiet neighbourhood. The man himself, eager to put his town on the map and ready to assume some bragging rights for running a tight ship, agreed immediately.

It was a clear, warm morning when the photograph was scheduled. Sheriff Anthony Miller was awake at five a.m., as was his usual fashion, so he could have a mug of hot coffee before the sun rose. His day began when the day began, he liked to say, and he wanted a moment of respite before another gruelling shift of patrolling an empty neighbourhood and speaking sternly to anyone thinking of littering. It was all about to pay off.

Coffee finished, he pulled his freshly ironed uniform out of the closet, sheriff badge polished and gleaming. He gave his neat room - bed made, desk dusted, bookshelf organised by colour - a once over. He didn't think the photographer would want any insider pictures, but better safe than sorry. There was a knock at his door.

"Comin'," he called out, gently laying out the uniform on his bed. Miller had put in the time to establish himself as a trusted pillar of the community, and it was common for him to get home calls, although not usually this early.

Sheriff Miller opened his door, the sun casting golden rays off of the rifle held by a small child whose eyes were the yellow of a coyote. Confusion wrinkled his brow as a bullet pierced his chest, knocking him flat on his back. The child, barefoot, stepped over him, unbothered. Miller coughed up blood, gasping for air, crimson staining his undershirt. Setting the rifle down on his desk, the child kicked his legs out of the doorway, closing and bolting the door. The child stepped onto his chest, ignoring Miller's whimpers of pain, and crouched down, face inches away from the sheriff's. His features, rippling like leaves in a summer wind, contorted and moulded until they were two perfect copies staring at each other. He stood up, taller, the sheriff's height. Even the scar on his ankle from breaking it by falling out of a tree at seven years old was an identical replica. Miller grasped weakly for anything in reach, the bedpost, the wall, his boots, his vision dimming. The copy chuckled, the same laugh Miller's mother used to tell him would break hearts.

"Don't make me shoot you between the eyes," it said in his voice, wandering over to his bed. Its fingertips stroked the badge as the light in the Sheriff's eyes went out and his choking breaths stopped.

Two hours later, the new sheriff was taking his place of pride in the centre of the photograph, the police station behind him. His deputy stood at his right hand side, the two of them beaming ear to ear. It was like that morning had never happened - like there wasn't a body soaking in hydrochloric acid in his tin bathtub.

There was a bright burst of flash, the photograph taken, the sheriff's face kept in a snapshot. It would be printed out, put in the paper, in a place of pride on the police mantlepiece. The sheriff would be remembered, revered. He had made it.

Tyler pulled the car into a side road off the very top of main street, barely more than an overgrown and secluded driveway. It used to lead to a hotel, but with the tourist business in Lovely long dead and buried, the building had itself been abandoned. The roof caved in during a thunderstorm twenty years ago, flooding the floors and whatever wasn't washed away rotted soon after. Now it hid, barely off the main road, a gutted shell of what used to be a dream destination. Even the rumours of it housing a chandelier were lost to the passage of time.

"Okay, so you check the library, okay? Find that folklore book printed out in the unit, any other information. I can come over tonight and we'll talk it over," Tyler said as he stopped the car. This way, no one in town could see them together.

"Don't come over. I can meet you at the bridge, or something." Heather had one hand on the car door, backpack already in her lap.

"Why can't I come over?"

"My dad would lose his mind, you know that. I'll meet you wherever you want."

"Can I at least pick you up?" He seemed to be genuinely asking. It still felt like a trap.

"Sure, and then we can make friendship bracelets and have sleepovers. You're ridiculous." She slammed the door, a little harder than expected. She was hiking the small hill to cut through the woodland before she could see whether he watched her leave or not.

Eric Kline had first started working at the library six years ago, aged seventeen. He had hated school - a scrawny, black-clad kid with two lip piercings and shaky eyeliner was not the most popular, surprisingly - and had no interest in his subjects or assignments. He spent most of his time in class at the back, scribbling angry poems in a battered notepad, avoiding eye contact and pretending he was anywhere else while also ignoring the steady stream of failing grades. Home wasn't much better - a pile of dirty dishes against stained lime green linoleum, his parents screaming so loudly it shook the glass panes in the back door, the television tuned to static. He would lie in bed, music playing quietly, staring up at the ceiling and thinking of new escape routes.

Then summer came, and his options were to sit within the same four walls of his room and let the floorboards slowly drive him crazy, or get a job. The gas station near his house was run by his father, so that was out of the question, and he didn't have his licence, which stranded him to either the Smith's auto shop or the library. His lab partner's name was Smith, and he hadn't been to that class in four weeks. That helped narrow it down.

He walked into the library on the first day of summer. The girl behind the front desk was cute - a dark fringe, blue eyeshadow, purple lipstick offset with a cream blouse. It was enough for him to ask for a job application. He filled it out on one of the oak benches, in red ink. Under *experience*, he put "conflict resolution".

Within a week, there was a phone call for him with an offer. Forty-five hours a week, minimum wage. He took it.

At first, he hated the job. Most of it was spent figuring out the backwards system of organising books, refiling returns, and arguing with customers who were so certain they were right. Multiple times, Eric stormed to the employee break room, confident he was going to quit that same night. He would always be there to open the next morning, no matter what.

By his second year there, the customers had become a steady lull, and the shelf was more easy to read. He became one of the fastest stockers, and just by telling him the genre of a book he could narrow down the aisle. Eric was a customer favourite, a town staple customers used to locate their favourite books. Sure, he had very mean nicknames for most of his regulars, but those he only said very quietly.

Six years after his first year, and four years after his high school graduation - no cords, certificate reluctantly given to him - he was an assistant manager. His boss, Joseph Tase, liked him a lot, and that was enough to carry him through the next few months of post-education employment. By then, he had saved enough to rent a small apartment above a pharmacy a few bends off main street. Sure, he did not own a second pillow, but he certainly did own an extensive liquor collection and a pack of smokes. Now, he knew the library like the back of his hand. He still wore all black and showed up five minutes late most days, but there was a shiny plastic badge pinned to his chest with his name on it.

Today was a shift like any other. Someone had stocked a fantasy sequel in nonfiction, the restock cart was almost overflowing, one of the helpdesk employees called out. But it was a slow day, so no real damage. Eric was reorganising a shelf, half-heartedly dusting, humming a metal song. He needed to laminate and label a new shipment of books, and then it was lunch.

The shift sped by. He ushered out the last few patrons at their seven p.m. close, told the other staff to go home, and turned his headphones up all the way as he finished up. The lights in the breakroom and stock cupboards got shut off, the last restocks put away, the trash bins by the customer desk and study tables emptied out. He swept and mopped the main entrance - the shelves, if he was thorough enough, only needed doing once a week - before turning out each individual desk lamp and shutting off the main lights. Eric sighed, giving the library one final look.

There was a light on in the very back hallway. He could have sworn he'd turned it off - but it had been a long night. If you close enough times, all the shifts blend into one, and you can find yourself mopping the same floorboard six times if you're not careful. It had happened to him before.

He made it to the back of the hall, shutting the light off. Eric picked his way back up, avoiding any damp patches where the floorboards hadn't had a chance to dry yet, picking up his backpack from its space by the front door. He turned around out of habit - and a desk lamp on one of the tables was switched on.

This time, Eric knew he had turned it off. He strode towards it, unease prickling in his spine. The switch *clicked* reassuringly under his index fingers, the lamp going dark. It was off. He was just tired. He would be home soon, in his cheap, empty apartment where the linoleum tiles on the wall didn't line up and the tap dripped the whole night. He reached the front door again, gripping the keys attached to his belt, turning around to expect darkness.

The light in the back hallway was on again. His hands squeezed into fists to stop the shaking. It was a power surge, or some faulty lightbulb, or some issue in the wires that snaked around the skeleton of the building, he knew it. There was a fast way to fix this.

Boots crunching into gravel, he rounded the outside of the building, to the rickety wooden shed on the other side of the parking lot. He unlocked the heavy metal padlock, pulling open the door and grabbing the flashlight on the workbench next to him. The fusebox let off a cloud of dust when he pulled it open, smacking every single switch to *off*. Eric twisted around, watching the building behind him fall into darkness.

Satisfied, he locked the shed up, testing the padlock twice. He rounded the corner, sliding the key into the lock and pulling the door shut. He looked up, out of instinct.

Every single light in the building was switched on. All the desk lamps, the overhead lights, the old sconces on the walls he had never seen lit. The library was a glowing beacon, almost too bright to look at. And there, far up against the back wall, was a man in a suit and tie.

Eric yanked his key out of the door, wrenching it open so fast it shook the wooden frame.

"Hey! We're closed!" He yelled, pissed that this was some practical joke, some stupid dare to keep him here late. He hated this job.

The man inside didn't move. Eric stepped inside, arms folded, keys jingling.

"Sir, you need to leave."

The man took a step towards him, polished leather on freshly cleaned tile. Eric should drag the mop over it again, but he was tired and annoyed. The stranger took another step, and then dropped to all fours, galloping towards him. He cleared the library in a matter of seconds, and it almost seemed as if his teeth were growing larger as he got closer.

"What the-" Eric managed before the man crashed into him, taking him through the door and flat on his back in the gravel lot. He looked up, and in the backlit glow the stranger's teeth seemed canine, animalistic, too big for his mouth. His eyes seemed to glint yellow - and then huge, fist-sized talons were ripped through Eric's shirt, his torso, cracking open his ribcage. The strangers' arms, rippling muscle and slight feathers, dug into him, lifting his glossy organs to its mouth. It hurt. He thought he could hear wings flapping as the corners of his vision went dark.

As Eric lay there, splayed on the gravel lot, arms weakly struggling against the thing sat on his chest feasting on his organs, he didn't think of his parents, who lived five minutes away and he hadn't spoken to in six months. He thought about how he was supposed to open tomorrow morning, and who would take on the job instead. Probably his manager, but maybe one of the new employees, if they happened to show up early. He was the only other key holder, and Joseph was worried about giving out any more copies. He thought about the shipment of new books that was coming in next week, on the early truck shift, and about how Mr Meclome would be there tomorrow, on his weekly visit, demanding an answer to a riddle he had made up and a new scientific journal to pour over. Eric looked up at the starless sky, listening to the dull crack of the vertebrate in his spine being wrenched apart, and thought about the patch of floor he hadn't gotten a chance to mop.

Heather was smoking by the bridge when Tyler picked her up. She finished her cigarette, watching him drum his fingers on the steering wheel while she made him wait. It was the little things.

"Hey," she finally opened the passenger seat door, her heavy backpack dropped on the floor.

"Hey," he started the car, headlights low in the dark.

"Where do you want to go? I think the diner will be open, but it's a little out of town, and-"

"We can just go to my place," he shrugged, his expression calm.

Panic rose in her throat. "What? No, I can't- I don't think-"

"Relax," he rounded the corner onto Main Street, which was hardly crowded at ten p.m. at night. If you were to sneak out, the only well-lit location wasn't exactly your first port of call. "My mum's passed out in a vermouth-induced sleep, and my father is spending the night at the office. No one will realise."

She nodded once, eyes glued to the passenger seat window.

"What about you? Your dad know you're out?"

"No, he's gonna be asleep until morning."

"How can you tell?"

"I put sleeping pills in his whiskey."

Tyler laughed. She wasn't joking.

He was right about the house, though. There was a light on in the hallway, and the front porch was lit up yellow, but other than that the house was silent. The door swung open when Tyler first tried it, the yellow tulips on the side table in the hallway wilted. Heather padded up the stairs behind him, tensing every single time one creaked. No one came to check on the noise. She waited until he shut his door behind them and turned the radio onto a low hum before taking her shoes off.

"No one's going to hear anything, don't worry," Tyler shrugged, pulling the light blue blinds closed and collapsing onto his bed. Heather sat cross legged on his floor, ripping open her backpack and letting the mess of loose paper fan out over the carpet. It was a collection of paper scans, transcripts, clippings. A small museum of weird happenings in their town. She unzipped the front pocket, pulling out a mostly full bottle of whiskey and a sealed can of diet soda, offering both to Tyler.

"Rough day?" he scoffed, grabbing an old glass from the stash of cups on his bedside table. He poured in a half shot, watching the soda fizzle on top.

"No, why would you ask?" She joked, chugging the whiskey straight from the bottle. He watched her for a moment, head propped up on his arms, before balancing the soda can on the table.

"So, the folklore wasn't very clear," she passed him some pages she had printed, then highlighted, then scribbled all over, then highlighted her scribbling. Some pages were more legible than others. "But there's a lot of legends about something in the woods. Like an evil creature lurking there and stealing children, or brings them back wrong, changeling style."

"Right," Tyler said, flipping through illustrations of birds with human hands and squirrels with canines, as if this was a normal way to spend his night. "So do you think-"

The phone rang - the one in his room, nestled on his desk between haphazard books and loose notes. It had gotten worse since she'd last been here. Heather twisted around to look at it, watching it ring again and again. Tyler set down the papers, picking his way around her, drink still in hand.

"Hello?"

She could hear a voice on the other end, a girl, talking fast.

"Hey, Annie," Tyler leaned back against the desk, swilling the dark liquid in his cup. Heather pretended to sort out the paper on the floor, feeling like she was the one intruding.

"Yeah, look, this isn't the best time-"

The voice on the phone got louder, more agitated. Heather kept her eyes on the floor.

"No, obviously I'm alone- I'm not-"

Her cheeks flared. She took another swig of whiskey. *I'm not here. This isn't happening. It's just the television on in the background.*

"Look, I'll call you back, okay?"

Muffled protests on the other end. Tyler sighed, not loud enough for the speaker to pick it up.

"I promise, alright? I'll call you back. Okay. Bye."

She heard the soft *thump* of the receiver being dropped down, the sound of him swallowing. More whiskey. She thumbed through the stack of papers.

Tyler circled her, sitting back down on his bed. He finished his drink.

"Sorry about that, I-"

"You don't have to be sorry, you don't-"

"No, honestly-"

Heather stood up, dropping the notes into his lap. "Look, you have all the information I could find. Read over it, let me know what you think whenever you're next free. I should go home anyway."

"Come on, don't."

Heather grabbed her backpack and the bottle, shoving on her shoes. The walk home would be good, and she could take some time for herself.

"Please don't leave."

She turned. Tyler was still on the edge of the bed, hand gripping the blanket so hard his knuckles were turning white. He wasn't looking at her.

"Nights are hard right now," he said, barely audible over the radio. "No one else will come over. Please stay."

She paused, fingertips lingering on the doorknob. Her backpack hit the floor.

"Okay."

Half an hour and most of the whiskey later, the two of them were stretched out on the bed, notes left on the carpet. She was trying really hard not to laugh at nothing.

"This is ridiculous though, right? Like this whole situation is insane," Tyler stumbled out, eyes closed. His arms were tucked behind his head, and it was almost possible to pretend the circles under his eyes were from end of term stress or breaking curfew too many times.

"Oh, this is the weirdest. I'm a little worried we're both losing it." She watched the ceiling spin, woozy and liking it.

"Hey, at least we're losing it together." Tyler opened his eyes, turning his head to look at her. She was still looking up, hands fiddling with the belt loops of her jeans.

"Hey," he said, quieter. His hand brushed against her cheek, then tucked a strand of hair behind her ear. Gentle.

"What?" she asked, turning to look at him. Her mouth grazed his fingers.

"Thank you for being here tonight. Honestly," he inched closer to her, his hands curling around her waist.

"Don't mention it," she shrugged, trying her best to stay still as he rested his head on her chest. He entwined one of his hands with hers.

"And this whole monster thing-"

Heather sighed dramatically, throwing her hands up. "Do *not* get me started on the monster thing."

He laughed. "We have to talk about the monster thing!"

"Okay, okay." She laughed at him through her words. Somehow, one of her hands ended up cradling his face. "If we're right about the monster thing-"

"Which we are."

Her hand slipped down, covering his mouth. A reflex, not a big deal.

"*If*, then how has no one even noticed this? Shouldn't there be an investigation about this? I mean, how are we the ones figuring this out? There's nothing special about us."

Tyler twisted, his hand sliding under her sweater as he brought his face inches from hers. "I think you're special."

Heather laughed. "I think you're full of shi-"

His phone rings. Tyler jolted, bolting upright. He stared at it for a second.

"Go answer it," Heather dropped her arms over her face. "I hate that sound."

"Okay!" Tyler scrambled over to his desk, picking up the phone and trying very hard to remember what being sober sounded like. "Hello?" Nailed it.

It was Annie, again. "Tyler? I didn't wake you, did I? I know it's late but I felt bad that my parents wouldn't let me come over and I figured you would still be awake and-"

"Yeah, 's fine. I'm up." He twisted around, the phone cord tangling around him, looking over to Heather on the bed. She looked almost comfortable. He winked at her.

"Okay nice! I just wanted to call and check up on you and- are you drunk?"

"Hm? What, no. 'm sober." He did not sound at all convincing.

"Okay, I get that things are rough for you right now or whatever, but I don't think getting *drunk* alone in your room is the best way-"

"I'm not alone," Tyler scoffed, "Heather's right here."

The line was silent for a moment.

"What the fuck?" Heather pushed herself up onto her elbows, the blood rushing to her head. Everything spun. Dread pooled in her stomach.

"Did you say Heather?" The neighbourhood could hear the disdain in Annie's voice. "Like, doesn't talk to anyone and tries to kill herself and is never in school Heather? Why the *fuck* would you be-"

"I gotta go," he mumbled, letting the receiver slip in his hand. It took him three tries to hang up properly, Annie's voice still sounding from the other end. He stood there, frozen.

Fuck. Heather pushed herself upright, dragging her hands through her hair. "I should go, I don't-"

"No, please-"

She staggered off the bed, tripping on her own feet. The room was a blur. "I shouldn't have-"

Tyler caught her, hands on her shoulders. She wouldn't look him in the eye.

"I should go home. This was a mistake-"

"Please," he blurred out, "please, please stay. I know I messed up, but I don't-"

"No, it's better if no one knows that we- you're right to-" The room was spinning, blurry. She wanted it to stop.

"Just sit down for a second, okay?" He tried. "Just a moment."

Heather nodded, letting him guide her back to the bed. She squeezed her eyes shut, resting her head on his shoulder, as if they were almost normal.

Tyler held her, trying to blink through the alcohol haze, trying not to think about how nice it felt and how badly he may have ruined it. "Please just stay here tonight. I don't care who knows. I'll do anything. I just can't keep being in this house alone."

It was silent for a moment, and then Heather rolled backwards, nestled into the blankets. "Fine. But you're making me coffee in the morning."

While it was almost definitely the late hour and the alcohol and the sheer relief, Tyler beamed. Actually beamed, his cheeks aching a little. "Deal. Anything you want."

She mumbled something, dragging a pillow down under her head. He gently rubbed her back, the way his father used to rub his mum's back after dinner, in the glow of the television, before his father slept with his secretary and his mum began unwinding with a bottle of vermouth and two olives. There was a moment of silence and then Heather, quiet and almost muffled - "Can you help me get my jeans off?"

When Madeline, aged twenty-four and married for three blissful years, learnt she was pregnant, she had a dream so vivid that when she woke up she forgot her name. In the dream, she was lying on a bed of crushed rose petals, watching clouds swirl through her hair and her nails melt into mist. There was water trickling somewhere near her, almost a babbling brook, and the heady scent of jasmine in the air. She felt a flutter by her wrists, and when she looked down, two giant white rabbits were sat on her legs, red eyes staring at her, sharp teeth on the skin of her wrists. Teeth nibbling through her flesh, her tendons, her veins, her bones. And she realised she was laughing, true peals of laughter so strong they brought tears to her eyes and trembled her shoulders. And she woke up, and once she had remembered her name, she turned to her husband and told him she was having twins.

Throughout her pregnancy, Madeline knew it would be twins. She demanded doubles of everything, painted the nursery in pink and eggshell white stripes, embroidered mirrored rabbits onto blankets and pillows and hats and nightgowns. When the time came to go to the hospital, she sternly told the doctor not to stop when the first baby was born - it was twins, and she would be leaving the ward with both of her babies.

Eight hours later, her face tear streaked and all of her husband's knuckles cracked from squeezing so hard, it was time. Madeline pushed and, as the valium settled in and the lights in the room blurred, she watched herself push out two beautiful rabbits. She heard their two peals of laughter, children's voices coming from behind those rodent teeth, and her eyes rolled back and exhaustion claimed her.

When Madeline woke up, clad in a paper-thin nightgown, the first words out of her mouth were "my babies". Her husband, tired, disheveled, scrambled out of his chair, standing between her and the cots in the room. He swayed on his feet for a moment.

Again. "My babies."

"My darling, you were right. It was twins, as you knew all along, somehow you-"

What was he talking about? She didn't care about any of this. "My babies."

"Madeline, please." Desperation and irritation mixing in his voice. "You were right, but there was a complication during the birth, and-"

A cry from behind him. Not a peal of laughter, but a wail, something piercing that shook her. She lifted her arms out, a silent demand.

"Alright. Madeline," her husband conceded. "But only one of our children survived. The other was stillborn. Do you understand?"

She was shaking her head. No no no no no. She heard two laughs. Her babies had made it. Her beautiful rabbits were alright.

Her husband gently lowered their child, swathed in pink silk and white cotton, into her arms. She could see the trembling in his arms but it didn't matter to her. Madeline held out her other arm, ready to cradle both of her babies at once.

"No, darling," her husband whispered, wrapping both of her arms around the child. He was wrong, but that was nothing new. He'd been wrong for the last nine months.

Madeline looked down at the baby in her arms, staring back up at her with pale white flecks of hair and red eyes, and smiled. If she could love one of them so much, she couldn't imagine how much love she would feel for two. Her husband's speech became a radio playing in a far away room.

"Bunny," she said.

Throughout their four day stay in the hospital - routine procedure for a stillbirth - Madeline kept demanding to see her second baby. She was so certain she had delivered two, two babies, and her arms felt empty only holding one child. She was built to carry the two of them. Nurses on the maternity ward developed a habit of carrying newborn babies upstairs, through the third floor of the hospital, and back downstairs, rather than carrying the swaddled child past Madeline's ward - she was at risk to steal a baby, the rumour was, given her insistence another child was owed to her.

When she finally left the hospital, escorted by her husband, Madeline made it halfway through the car park before the panic set in. Her other child was in the hospital, she knew. They were keeping her baby from her. They had taken her, her precious child with crimson eyes and hair like freshly fallen snow, stolen her child and deceived her husband.

It took four orderlies and a near-lethal injection of anaesthetic to get her into the car. Her husband was handed a pill bottle and a repeat prescription, told to phone if there were any further problems. He drove her home, tucked her into bed, installed a latch on the outside of their bedroom door. He held their daughter, who didn't cry, only reached one hand out to her mother's sleeping body.

Seven weeks of bedrest and medication-induced delirium later, Madeline was back to her old self. She dismissed her actions as labour related confusion, returned to her neighbourhood walks and embroidery, dutifully swallowing her prescription every morning. Her husband was so relieved to have his wife back, the woman that baked apple pies and read to their child and darned his socks, that he ignored the times she would stare listlessly into their back garden, letting a pot of soup boil over and burn.

Before either of them knew it, Bunny was seven years old, in school. Bright, friendly, smiling so wide it made stranger's cheeks hurt, she was Madeline's pride and joy. She would skip home, Madline walking patiently at her side, chattering about her exploits, two long white-blonde plaits swinging behind her. Her father would pat her head at dinner, interrupt her to remind her to eat the chicken on her plate, jokingly offer her a sip of bourbon. Madeline would purse her lips, but she was happy.

Then, one night. Bunny was nine years old, the lead in the school play, the fridge blanketed in A+ homework assignments. Madeline cannot sleep - no matter how much she tossed, how much she paced, no matter how many of the little pills she swallowed, she was awake, glaring at the walls. Her husband slumbered beside her, unaware of her turmoil. Finally, Madeleine abandoned sleep. She hummed, scrubbing down the kitchen counters, drying dishes, dusting skirting boards. There was one singular lamp lit, and her steps feather-light, trying not to wake the rest of the house. A damp cloth polished the windows in the kitchen and there, in the dark of the back garden, two yellow eyes stared back at her.

Madeline looked away. She fumbled a glass of water from the cabinets and the sink, pried open her bottle of clarity pills, spilled six too many of them into her hand. Took them all. Drops of water on the kitchen tiles, need to clean that later. Looked back into the garden - the eyes, closer now. She felt calmer.

She turned on the light by the backdoor, unlocked it, swung it open. In the back garden, illuminated by an artificial light, was a small girl, crouched in the grass. Her golden blonde hair fell in straggly knots, and her long white rabbit ears perked up at the movement in the house. She looked back at Madeline with piercing scarlet eyes.

She didn't know if it was a maternal instinct, or the late hour, or too many prescription pills, but she stepped into the back garden. The stones of the patio were rough and cold under her bare feet, and the night breeze chills her. But she crouched down, holding out her arms to the rabbit-girl. Whispered *bunny*. And the girl bounds - no, hops - across the wet lawn and into her arms. Pressed her damp nose into the crook of Madeline's necks. Burrowed into her chest.

The next morning, her husband wakes up to cold daylight and a blaring alarm clock. He stirs, and then the smell of wet grass and rot hits him. Madeline is curled up next to him in the bed, her feet muddy, her shoulders damp. He shook her awake, roughly, and when she sat up there was a huge white rabbit cradled in her arms, pink nose twitching.

For the first time in her young life, Bunny woke up to shouting. She padded out to see her parents in the kitchen, her father's work shirt untucked and creased, her mother's turned back. No sign of breakfast on the table.

"Have you lost your mind?" Her father yelled. "We are not keeping it!"

"It's mine!" Her mother snapped, still staring out the window. "You have no right!"

"No right?!" Her father threw his hands up. "I am calling your doctor, today. The medication clearly isn't working anymore. If I knew you would react like this, I would-"

"You would what?" There was a cruelty in her mother's voice she hadn't heard before. "Leave me in that hospital? Let my Bunny rot there with me?"

"Jesus, Madeline!" Her father snapped, finally looking up to his daughter lingering in the hallway. She watched him attempt to compose himself, smoothing down his hair and his shirt collar. "Morning, Bunny," he tried feebly.

Madeline turned around at this, the checkered yellow of her dress swinging, and Bunny saw the large white rabbit cradled in her arms. Her mother beamed at her.

"Good morning, sweetie. I'll make you something in a moment, alright?"

Bunny took a step into the kitchen, reaching out a hand. "Is that for me?" Her mother kept smiling, but there was a hardness in her eyes now. "No, darling. This is my rabbit. It's not a pet for you."

"Oh." Bunny's eyes crinkled, almost watering. "I thought-"

"No," her mother's voice was gentle, but there was a sense of urgency in her words. "Why don't you go and get dressed, and breakfast will be ready soon."

Sure enough, fifteen minutes later there was toast and eggs and bacon and orange juice on the table. Her father sat and sipped his coffee, pretending to read a newspaper. Madeline still cradled the rabbit in her arms, feeding it carrot sticks. She didn't seem to notice when Bunny dribbled yolk on her shirt, or dusted her skirt with crumbs. She didn't look up when her father left for work.

The clock in the hallway read 8.30 when Bunny finished tying her shoes, schoolbag in hand. Madeline was sat on the sofa, television on, whispering into the rabbit's ear. For the first time in her young life, Bunny felt an ugly twinge of jealousy.

"We're going to be late," she tried, shifting uncomfortably on the rug. "Mum-"

"Now, Bunny," Madeline sighed, as if what she was going to say next greatly pained her to announce. "You're a big girl now, and I think it's about time you walked to school by yourself. You're a bright girl, and you know the way, don't you?"

She did know the way, and the school was barely a fifteen minute walk from the house, although neither of these facts especially mattered to Bunny in the moment.

"But you always walk me."

"I know, darling." The smile slid off her mothers face. "And today, you're walking by yourself."

Bunny cried through her lessons, all the way to lunchtime when a teacher finally pulled her aside and asked what was wrong. The four calls to her home went unanswered, and the phone call placed to her father's office reached a secretary who had been told he was not to be disturbed. Bunny's teachers assumed her mother would arrive at the end of the day, and all of this would be put to rest, choosing to send her back to class with a consolation chocolate bar. When the final bell rang, and there was no Madeline at the gates, they phoned the police.

A team of three police officers were sent to Madeline's house, and hammered on the front door. No one answered - the front door was unlocked. The television was playing to any empty living room, and what looked like a picked-at vegetable platter sat on the coffee table. An officer made his way upstairs, swinging open the door to the master suite, where he found what was left of Madeline - her flesh torn through, teeth marks on her very bones. Grass and leaves and blood on the rug.

The coroner's office ruled it an animal attack, an unfortunate thing that occasionally happens in small towns. Bunny's father burnt down the house that night, and drove the two of them until they were in a city too big to see the trees. It took four years for Bunny to speak again, and she never owned a pet rabbit.

Chapter Six

In the early mornings, on the nice side of town where the Henderson's lived, the sunlight streamed through a fan of leaves and flowers. The bright light settled on thick carpet, reflecting off of hardwood floors. It's the kind of morning that makes you want to stay under the covers - not to avoid the world, but to stay basking in the radiance of it all for a moment more.

Heather found this out by waking up with a splitting headache, her throat dry, drool on the pillow below her. It was glaringly bright, and she blinked like a deer in the headlights.

There was a weight on her back. She twisted, muscles protesting. Tyler was fast asleep, his head on the ridges of her spine, his arms around her waist, their legs twisted together. Her jeans were flung onto the floor, along with the sweater she had been wearing, but her vest and underwear were stuck with sweat to her skin. Tyler was still fully clothed, his hair a mess, gently snoring.

She twisted further, glancing at the clock on his desk. 5:05. She probably had another hour until her dad woke up, maybe two if she was lucky. That didn't mean it wasn't time for her to leave.

Heather shimmied out from under Tyler, pushing him onto the pillows and crawling out of his bed. Her mouth was unbelievably dry. She dropped a blanket onto him, dragging on her clothes and shoes. Backpack on, she reached for the door handle, casting one glance back at Tyler - and heard the sound of a television switching on somewhere else in the house.

She froze. Despite being over a multitude of times over the last two years, she had never been here when anyone else was home. She didn't know the exits, or if the window opened. Heather wasn't a deer in the headlights - she was a rat in a glue trap.

"Tyler?" she grabbed his shoulder, shaking him awake, hard. "Tyler, come on."

"Wha?" he blinked, squinting in the light, eyes blurry. "What's going on?"

"Tyler, wake up, *now*." She shook his shoulder again, working really hard on keeping her voice down.

"Yeah, I'm up," he sat up, stretching. "I'm up."

"Tyler, I need to go home."

He blinked at her.

"There's someone awake in this house. I need to leave."

"Ah," Tyler nodded. "Yeah, that's an issue."

Do not hit him. Heather crossed her arms. "Help?"

"Okay, okay. Sorry." Tyler stumbled to his feet, giving his head a quick shake. "Let me think."

"Can you cause a distraction? Or let me out the window? Or-"

"Or I can just walk you out the front door."

"What? You're not-"

"Don't shake me again," he threw up his hands. "I'm serious. I think I might be slightly hungover."

"You're ridiculous."

"No, honestly. I have friends over all the time, and it's not like my parents are really talking to anyone right now."

"I don't like it."

"I would owe you," he offered, forcing a smile.

"You already owe me for last night." She glanced at the clock. 5:23. Time to go. "Fine. But only because I have no other choice."

"You're a charmer, you know?"

Behind the Henderson's house, behind the whole cookie cutter neighbourhood, was a stretch of woodland separating the back gardens from the interstate three miles away. The trees glowed amber in autumn, frosted over in winter, blossomed in spring and spent the summer entwining their leaves for a patch of shade. Tyler and Max had built a den there as kids, decorated it with old bunting and rocks, sharpened sticks to defend it from imaginary foes. It was the patch of trees their neighbours would let their dogs run free through, children would play in, couples would pick as the location for evening strolls. At the odd barbecue, someone would mention expanding their lawn out into the brushland; but they never would. The woodland was too magical to ruin with a manicured patch of grass.

When Lovely was first founded, those trees hadn't been felled or pushed back or even trimmed. It was simple as to why - when the first axe bit into a flaky layer of bark, the roots of the tree rose up and pulled the limbs off of the man's body. It was a very effective deterrent.

For the next fifty years, those trees were shunned. People would swear they saw them shifting at night, rearranging, growing suddenly taller. Branches would move, spring out of nothing, crash down onto your neighbour's head. If you tried to leave through them, the forest would twist and squirm its way around you, spitting you out exactly where you started. Sometimes you would hear screams, or howling, or eerie, too-perfect silence.

But, as is true of everywhere, people forget. A cursed patch of land becomes attractive real estate you can use as a buffer between your new construction and the road. You can preserve it, and use it to drive up the prices. It's now an idyllic house, a new home where your children can be safe from the road. It's now a part of the illusion you are creating in one of the country's safest towns, where nothing bad ever happens.

And who would notice if a tree moves in the night every now and again, or if the neighbourhood pets keep going missing? Sure, there's never any birdsong or bugs or wild animals in those woods, but it is almost impossible to prove a negative. What child doesn't wake up screaming from nightmares of gnarled branches unlocking their window and creeping inside, wenching open their throats and unspooling their intestines through their mouth? It's not the kind of thing you would mention to your neighbour over cups of coffee or a shared barbecue, and it's just a regular part of growing up. This is a nice, normal neighbourhood, after all. You wouldn't want to be the one to ruin that, would you?

Please. What would the neighbours think?

When Heather used to come over to the Henderson's house - ages six to ten, usually for birthdays and end of term parties and the occasional pool day - it would always be in a gaggle of other children, tagging on as a whole class invite. She could skulk at the back of the group, avoiding eye contact with any adults, and feast on pastel cupcakes and savoury pastries until she heard her dad's car horn blaring from the road. At this point she would slink out, no *thank you*'s exchanged, usually with a small scented candle or teaspoon stashed in her jean pockets. Nothing that would be missed.

This time, however, she was the only non-family member standing on the bottom of the stairs, the whole limelight on her. She had tried to fix her hair, her creased sweater, herself. She did not think she'd been successful.

Tyler's mother was the one staring at her, clad in a rose pink dressing down with teal hair curlers loosely held in her dulling bleach job. There was a half-empty martini glass in her left hand.

"Hello," she said flatly, leaning back against the living room door frame. The television was on, the weather report rolling by. Only Tyler's car was in the driveway. "And you are?"

"Heather," she smiled weakly. "Heather Strand."

"Of course!" The smile Mrs Henderson gave her was not particularly warm or inviting. "It's always nice to meet one of Tyler's- well."

Tyler shifted next to her, visibly uncomfortable. He wasn't saying anything.

"And how is your father?"

"He's fine," Heather definitely wasn't rattled, and her nails were not biting into her palms. "Working a lot."

"Ah, of course. He was always a hard worker." She looked Heather up and down, at the threadbare knees of her jeans and the whiskey stains on her sweater. "He'd have to be, given your family's-"

"Mum, we should go." Tyler smiled at her, grimly, already pulling on his shoes.

"Honey, I'm just saying," his mother sighed out, taking another sip of her glass. The gin wafted through the hallway, curdling in Heather's hungover stomach. "Where are you rushing off to anyway? It's so early. Stay for breakfast."

"Mum, please," Tyler slammed the opening door into the hallway wall, making Heather jump. She nodded, her pathetic excuse for a smile never slipping, and scampered after him. Mrs Henderson watched the car leave, swaying in the doorway, distaste wrinkling her nose. For just a moment, Heather wished she could bring up her own mother, mention a moment when she was just as embarrassing and caring and endearing.

Heather made him stop the car just off Main Street, insistent on walking.

"Call me?" he asked, hopeful. Heather was trying very hard not to openly sigh at him.

"I will. Have fun in school." She pushed open the door.

"You could always come to school? We have class together after lunch. No tests."

"Maybe," she faked a smile. "I'll see."

"Sure," he nodded, watching her swing the backpack onto her shoulder. Just before she got out of the car, he leaned forwards and kissed her on the cheek. It made her stomach coil, but that may have been last night's alcohol.

Tyler made it back to and out of the house with no complications - still no sign of his father, and his mum was back to snoozing on the sofa, gin martini spilling onto the shag carpet. He spent the first three hours of classes in the student car park, drumming his fingers on the steering wheel and changing radio stations. *Ten more minutes and then you have to go inside*, repeated for the billionth time. It took until lunch time for him to grace the hallways with his presence.

He grinned at his friends - most of which were on their way to peeling out of school for a precious hour of respite - as he made his way to the administrative office. Shirley, who worked the desk until the afternoon, waved him off, already leafing through attendance logs with a marker in hand. Her fudging his participation grades was one of the few reasons he was not currently failing.

In his mind, school was currently a series of cheats and favours he was going to coast until summer, when he would get his shit together and come back as an actual academic. Or at least, that was what he was telling himself. As long as he kept things afloat for the next three weeks, he would be okay. He was a good student, normally, and as long as he kept selling that charade with enough charm and confidence, it was something teachers would want to believe.

He pushed open the door to his biology class room, all burnt, chipped wooden benches and potential gas leaks. Miss West was sitting at her desk, polished plastic red apple in front of her, crescent wire glasses perched on her head. She was in the middle of marking a stack of test papers in a red marker that was staining her hands and polka dot blouse.

"Miss?"

She perked up, grey eyes squinting at him. "Tyler! Good afternoon! How are you?"

Chipper, as always. No response to his absence that morning, or the last two weeks of silence in classes and half-finished homework assignments. "Not bad. How are you?"

"Coffee exists, so no complaints here," she beamed, already rifling through her desk drawer. Her organisation system, whatever it was, seemed like a nightmare - and yet, the paper he had been looking for had appeared in her hand. "Today's homework, due next week."

He gave her his well-practised smile, tucking the pages under his arm. "Thank you. I'll get it to you by then."

"No hurry, Tyler. You have a good weekend." Her tone was genuine, but she was already back to her marking, red ink spilling over someone else's scribbles.

"Thank you," he nodded, ducking back out of the classroom.

His next stop was the library, a glorified barn crammed with shifting shelves behind the gym. It was also the preferred lunch spot of his English teachers, a quiet refuge for loud gossip. Tyler crossed the courtyard to it, a second of sunlight, and his hand was on the library door when someone called his name.

He turned - blonde hair, freckles, denim skirt and knee high socks. Annie. Shit.

"Hey," he tried, tucking his hands into his jeans pockets. "Long time no see."

"Yeah, I'm sorry," she smiled up at him, one hand playing with the end of her plait. "My grades dropped over spring break and my parents have been so on me for studying, it sucks. I mean, I know they just want the best for me but I want a social life too, you know? It's not like one night away from home is going to tank my finals, right?"

"Right." He hated it, but there's really no way to respond to Annie that doesn't feel like you're interrupting. "Anyway, I should-"

"Also, I'm so glad I saw you because I really wanted to talk to you. Were you really with Heather last night? I mean, I don't want to sound like I'm judging you because we're friends so I'm totally not, but are you sure-"

"It's not a big deal," Tyler tried, casting an intentional glance at the library.

"I obviously haven't told anyone, but like wouldn't it make things weird at school? Given her history, and you're such a good student, and I don't-"

"Annie, I have to go, okay?" He held up his biology homework, the paper a white flag of surrender.

"Wait!" She hugged him, tight, almost crumpling the page. He wondered if he still smelt like whiskey and Heather's cigarettes. "You never called me."

"I'll call you soon, okay?" He stepped back, squirming out of her grip. "I'm sorry, I just have a lot to get done."

"I'll see you in class!" She called, watching as disappeared into the dimly lit building. She was so telling Bethany about this.

Thirty minutes later and Tyler was in history, back of the class, an empty notebook in front of him. He did not want to be there - but this was one of the few classes where just textbooks couldn't help him. Desperate times.

Peter, on his left, was relaying the content of the last six classes, the collar of his light blue shirt wrinkled and a battered Shakespeare play battered on his desk. King Lear. Tyler was nodding at the right moments and pretending to read the notes on board, but his mind felt crammed full of cotton balls. The headache was not helping.

He watched the rest of the class file in, the bell silent - it had broken long before he started school - and finally his professor, almost late. Mr Smith was wearing at least four layers, despite the warm weather, and holding an Italian dictionary for an unexplainable reason. Tyler let himself zone out.

Ten minutes into Mr Smith's lecture - all of which was about the traffic this morning, and Tyler hoped was going to be on the exam - the door swung open and Heather slipped in. She was wearing the good navy sweater, the same pair of jeans as this morning, and a probably empty backpack. Bethany, two seats in front of him, twisted around to shoot him a puzzled glance. He fought to keep his expression blank. It was Heather's first time in school in three months - and she was in their history class.

He looked at the board, at the chalk Mr Smith was scrawling less than legibly. Heather had an old journal in front of her, blunt pencil moving across it. Not that he was staring.

The next hour of class was Tyler flicking between trying to subtly stare at Heather, who was continuously writing at the front of the class, at the board where Mr Smith's writing was now layered on top of itself and spilling out in circles, and avoiding Bethany's increasingly pointed glares. Peter raised his hand to inform Mr Smith that class had ended - any plans to repair the class bell had been buried under plumbing and lighting issues long before any of their parents had started studying there - and the class trickled out into the already swarming corridor. Heather was one of the first gone, her head down, bag still unzipped. By the time Tyler had queued and waited his way out of the room, he'd lost sight of her.

What the fuck was that.

He weaved his way down the halls, forcing a path away from his net class, slamming the outside door open. It bounced off the brick wall, almost mowing down a group of junior football players. He kept walking, cutting diagonally across the car park and climbing into his car. By school rules, there should have been a teacher or a chaperone watching to make sure no one drove during school hours, in case someone reversed into a student or, god forbid, a window. But hey, the week was almost over.

Tyler turned on his radio. He pulled open the glove compartment, sifting around in the vague hope Heather may have left a drink of something, anything, in his car. There were a few cigarette butts, an empty lighter, a charm bracelet he was ninety odd percent certain wasn't her's. *Fuck.*

It seemed like he would just have to sit here, in silence, and wait until she got back to tell him about her hiding spaces. What a shame.

Rose Appleton first fell in love aged 13, with the high school senior who mowed her family's lawn after school. She would lie, elbows propped up on the back of the sofa, gel pen scribbling in her pink journal, daydreaming of him. Him walking through the front door, sweeping her off her feet and carrying her away to a fairytale castle - or, more realistically, the coffee shop on Main Street her mother wouldn't let her visit. He left for college that same summer, effectively breaking her young heart in a way no prom date could.

Then, before even she knew it, Rose was eighteen, working at the ice cream parlour behind an almost run down bar. She was wiping down a counter permanently stained with chocolate fudge, counting down the clock until her shift was over, when Evan walked in the door, all blond confidence and fresh denim jeans. He gave her an easy, well-practised grin.

"Mornin'."

"Good afternoon," she gave him a tight-lipped, tired smile. She didn't mean it as a correction. "How can I help you?"

"Can I get two scoops of strawberry, please? In a cone."

"Of course," she turned her back, switching out a new silver metal scoop and picking up a cone. She turned back around, the bow strings of her pastel apron swinging by her sides. Evan was dropping a crisp ten dollar bill into the battered tip jar, his eyes locked to her.

"That's very generous, but you don't have to-"

"I can't help but tip the prettiest girl I've seen all day, now can I?" he grinned at her. Rose couldn't help it - she blushed. He left his phone number on a napkin, and the second she got home, she called it.

Their first date was at the coffee shop, where they shared pastries and talked about everything. He had picked her up, in a freshly pressed suit, bouquet of red roses in hand. Evan got her home one minute past her curfew - the one minute squandered in her driveway, his lips kissing her so gently it almost hurt. Rose deemed it worth it.

A year later - a year of sneaking stolen wine into sunset picnics, laughing through dinner dates, car rides that ended up in the back seat, hours in drive-in cinemas watching bad films - they were back in that coffee shop. Rose's hair was a little longer, her dress red silk, her cardigan white cashmere. She was the shift lead of the ice cream shop. They had an apartment together, cheap yellow walls on the edge of town. They were happy.

"You remember our first date here?" she asked, taking a sip of her cappuccino. He beamed at her, nodding.

Their selection of pastries and sandwiches - cranberry and brie, ham and cheese, pesto, strawberry jam, cream cheese, danish, chocolate - littered the table between them. Evan traded bites with her, drinking his own hot chocolate, his suit collecting flaky crumbs.

"You folks need anything else?" the waiter, freshly sixteen with a toothy smile and a smattering of freckles, asked, clutching a paper pad in his sweaty hand. Rose shook her head, smiling.

"We're fine, actually," Evan snapped.

Rose's eyes met his - blue, darkened. He was angry. She knew him - she woke up with his bare chest pressed against her, she washed his laundry, she cleaned up his dirty dishes and his vomit after his late nights at the bar. She knew what anger looked like on him.

Rose spent the evening surrounded by candlelight and fresh coffee and the baking of bread, begging him to tell her what was wrong. He was a brick wall. They finished their pastries and drinks, and walked into the dark night, Rose trailing behind him to their parked car. He unlocked it, sliding into the driver's seat and starting the engine. Shame burned at her cheeks as she made sure no one saw her open her own car door. They made the drive to their apartment in silence. Rose was in the bathroom, taking out her earrings, waiting for Evan to say anything.

That night, he hit her for the first time.

His fist struck her jaw as she walked out of the bathroom. *Why did you smile at him,* Evan screamed. *Why would you do that? Why did you make me hit you?*

The next morning, Rose woke up to cold sunlight and empty sheets. She blamed herself. She should be more careful.

The years that followed were more of the same. Incredible weeks and months that seemed out of a fairytale, magical spellbinding nights of red roses and chaste kisses - and then punches that broke her jaw, her nose, her wrist. Him screaming she was hurting him, betraying him, embarrassing him. Rose waking up alone.

By then, they had moved into a two-bedroom house in the suburbs, the kind with a back garden some kids could run around with. Evan was the love of her life, and she wouldn't carry his child. She had quit her job, cut ties with most of her friends, become a hollow husk of herself. Rose spent most of her days counting down the minutes until Evan got home, deep cleaning the house and experimenting with sour cream based salads. The happy pills from her doctor didn't hurt.

It was two days before their five year anniversary when Evan came home an hour late. Rose had spent the sixty minutes pacing their yellow linoleum kitchen, adjusting her braided hair, and sweeping their hallway. He staggered in, late, tiredness in his eyes.

"Hello, honey," he smiled, and her shoulders tensed instantly. He was never this nice, not in private. He placed a tender kiss on her cheek, then made his way to the table. Rose sat opposite him, hands gripping her thighs, scared.

Throughout that dinner, he was perfect - not normal, but perfect. He sang his praises of her honey roast ham, her garlic potatoes, her buttered green beans. He told her how nice this was to come home to at the end of a long day at work.

Rose was washing dishes when he came up to her. He lingered for just a second - and then he picked up a tartan tea towel, and began drying. Something Evan had never done. Rose did her best not to react.

Two days later, she was leaning on the doorway, talking to the kid that was offering to mow their lawn. He was tall, tawny blond, his polo shirt unbuttoned. Rose forgot herself, laughing at his jokes, admiring this sixteen year old's well paced sales pitch. He was writing down his phone number and address when her husband's car pulled into the drive. Fear raced down her spine. She ushered the kid out, panic rising in her throat.

Evan stepped out of the car, leather briefcase in hand. He waved goodbye to the boy, smiling as he walked up the pavement, clicking the door shut behind him. Rose looked at him, untensing her jaw so that it didn't break - a lesson she had learnt the hard way - and bracing her legs not to fall. He kissed her, oh so gently, on the cheek.

The whole of the evening, she wavered next to him, waiting for the other shoe to drop. It didn't - he loved her cooking, laid his head on her shoulder while they were watching television, and held her tight in bed. She was never once hurt. She almost felt loved. Almost like a love that belonged in those films she used to watch.

A week later - her first week without having to cover a bruise or heal a bleeding wound in what felt like forever - Rose was woken up in the night. It was too dark to see a time, but there was a sound coming from the back garden. The sheets next to her were cold.

Rose, hands trembling, crept up to the window, and snapped the curtains back. There, illuminated in the porch light she always left on, was her husband, hunched over the body of a deer, his mouth tearing off the flesh and gulping it down. She watched until she felt the bile rising in her throat.

Two hours later, not-Evan slid back into their cold bed, his feet still damp from the dew of their lawn. Rose, who was still awake, waited until his breathing slowed. And then, for the first time in just over five years, she rolled over and snaked one hand over his stomach. She wrapped a leg around his thighs. She pulled him closer to her.

The next morning - and each morning after - was bliss. not-Evan doted on her, worked hard on his office, treated her gently. Rose planted saplings in the back garden that attracted deer, perfected her steak recipe, fucked him until her eyes rolled back in her head. The two of them kept a low profile in the town - they won the occasional baking contest for a pot pie, but that was it. They were happy.

And, when Rose was tired, and strung out, and weary, not-Evan quit his job to care for her. He cooked chicken soups for her, cared for her every want, paced all night while she tossed and turned. This went on for several years - and when Rose did die, happy and safe in her own home, no one wept more than not-Evan at the funeral. And the next day, he walked into the woods, his pockets empty, his house fully furnished and yet abandoned. He didn't see the point of living without her. He just walked away - and as much as we know, he's still walking now.

Tyler's car was still in the school car park, engine idling, forty minutes after the last class ended. The school buses had pulled away, and most of the student body was long gone. Heather was leaning against someone else's locker, just inside the hallway. She was waiting for him to leave. He was probably waiting for her.

"Kid? It's hometime." The janitor, mop in hand, was stood next to her, his eyes tired. There was a faded red and black striped sweater under his blue overalls. Pink soap dripped onto the linoleum tile by her feet.

"I know. Sorry, Steve."

"No sweat," he was turning away, humming something under his breath.

Heather shoved open the metal doors, out into the car park. She forced her hands into her jean pockets, tucking her head down and striding towards the road. She got ten steps before Tyler's car rounded the curb in front of her.

Tyler lunged across the centre console to throw open the passenger side door. His radio was on, and there was a half done crossword on the dashboard. He'd been ready to wait for a while. "Get in!"

Heather scrambled in, slamming the door shut behind her. "You don't have to drive me home."

"Oh, I'm not," he grinned. "I want burgers and I've never been to Bunny's alone. I do have a reputation to uphold, you know?"

She rolled her eyes at him, dumping her bag on the floor. "I'm not the best dinner date."

"Please, you know you being in the car is more than enough, right?"

Bunny's was a burger place a ten minute drive away from Lovely, less if you broke the speed limit. The local rumor behind its slightly far out location - not quite committed to being a part of the town, not exactly separate - was that they tried to build it in the town, but every time the builders finished work for the day, they would return the next morning to find the bricks scattered, the doors pulled off their hinges, themselves back at square one. The first intersection south was the closest they could get to the town with the walls still standing.

It was a red and white tile, its food served in takeaway containers, the jukebox permanently and on purpose broken type of establishment. It was also Tyler's favourite, and he wasn't lying when he said he was a regular. The waiter behind the counter began work on a chocolate milkshake the moment he walked in the door. Heather lingered behind him, plucking a menu from a table and leafing through it. She was turning the pages a little too fast to actually be absorbing anything - it was one of her tells.

"Tyler! What can I do for you?" The waiter beamed, almost too friendly. Tyler didn't mind.

"Hey Mark," he pulled his wallet out of his back pocket. "Can I get a number three combo with a shake, an extra medium fries, and a coffee, black? To go, please."

"You got it, man," Mark began punching keys into the register. Heather dropped the menu back onto the table, face down, not making eye contact. Tyler would take care of it in the car.

He paid, tucking the brown paper bag of food under his arm and scooping up the drinks. Heather followed him out, ducking through the open door. They drove a short way back to Lovely, before Tyler pulled onto a side road that rounded a small hill, tapering off to a grassy patch that overlooked the town. You could see the whole town from up here, the glow of streetlights and house windows, far enough away that it was almost quiet. It was the closest thing they had to a lover's lane, not that anyone actually used it as such. He never took her there.

"Here," he passed her her coffee and one of the fries. She still wasn't looking at him, not that it surprised him.

Heather pulled the lid off the cup, reaching under the passenger seat to pull out a hip flask. Tyler watched dark liquid swirl in, resisting the urge to swear. *How many hiding places does she have?*

He had a brief, entertaining image of her filling his car with flasks, like a squirrel stashing acorns for the winter. Maybe one of them would grow into a tree, gushing whisky instead of sap.

"Hey," he took a slurp of milkshake, using the straw to push the whipped cream out of the way. "Share."

"You shouldn't drink and drive," she smiled, her tone a little scolding. She indulged him anyway.

"Here, I found something." Heather passed him the piece of paper, trading it for the container of fries. She picked one up. "Some camp, years ago. Sounds like it might be the kind of thing we're looking for. The counselor's still alive."

Tyler nodded, his eyes scanning the article. "Seems like it. How do you know she's still alive?"

Heather took a gulp of milkshake, letting it warm in her mouth for a second. Chocolate. "I called the asylum pretending to be a niece. They said she's accepting visitors."

"Wow." He paused for a second, eyeing his burger. She waited for him to look at her. "Impressive."

Heather shook her head, plucking the burger from his hand and taking a bite. Salted patty and ketchup and melted cheese. "Not really."

He laughed, swapping the fries in his hand for the burger. Heather finished the shake, propping her feet up next to his crossword. She almost leaned her head on his shoulder.

"I could get used to this," his voice was quieter than it normally was. He wasn't looking at her - he was watching the road down below, streaked with frequent car headlights. His hand found hers and gripped it. She didn't know what to say.

Tyler waited until the meal was empty containers littering his dashboard. "We should call it a night. It's a long drive tomorrow, and-"

"We?"

He rolled his eyes. "Fine, me. If I'm going to be driving the whole day, you don't want me to do it tired."

"Fine. Can you drop me off?"

He tried to hide it, but his hands faltered for a second. Tyler gripped the steering wheel to hide it. "What will your dad say?"

Heather rolled down the window, lighting up a cigarette. "I don't care."

Chapter Seven

The last time Heather saw her mother, it was seven sleeps until Christmas. Main Street had put up its decorations - a few meagre pieces of tinsel around the light posts and a cheaply decorated tree, but they'd driven down the street at a snail's pace even still. Heather had sulked in the back seat, wishing she had been allowed to go to a friend's party she no longer remembered the name of. She hadn't said a word, but her mother had been passing orange slices back to her. Heather watched the twinkling lights propped up in shop windows, the paper bags of shoppers, the groups of teenagers laughing over steaming hot chocolates. One day, she told herself, that would be her, giggling between mouthfuls of whipped cream and tossing back her perfectly curled locks.

That night, unbeknownst to her, three hours after she had fallen asleep her parents were decorating their living room. Her father was holding an annoyingly long stream of tinsel in both hands, a loop of it tied around his neck, grinning too wide in the photograph her mother snapped. Heather would find this photograph years later, slipped under the liquor cabinet among the dust and mothballs. She would hide it in her wardrobe. They were in their late twenties, him in flannel trousers and a loose t-shirt, her in a red sweater and his flannel trousers. The tree was up, scattered with baubles and paper fans, and there were cards standing up on the coffee table, threatening to fall like dominoes.

"Do you think she'll be upset we didn't let her help?" her mother asked, winding tinsel around a door handle.

"She's always upset these days," her father muttered, dropping tinsel down and picking up his beer.

"That's true." A longing gaze at the shut bedroom door down the hall. Neither of them could recall the last time she'd woken them up at night.

"Do you worry about her?"

Her father took a long gulp. "Worry about what? Her getting into trouble?"

"No," she half-laughed. She'd been doing that a lot recently. "Worry about how she's doing. It can be hard, growing up in this town, and I don't-"

"She's doing fine," he snapped. "Can we just enjoy the evening?"

A quiet, frustrated sigh. Hands on hips. "I don't think worrying about my daughter is going to-"

"*Your* daughter-"

"You know what I meant-"

Knocking at the door halted the argument. The two of them turned, staring at the metal latch.

Her mother turned to him, aware it was almost midnight, aware they didn't know any of their neighbours that well. The yellow lace curtain covering the window swayed a little.

Another knock, louder this time. Someone hammering on the front door she kept asking him to repaint. Her father grabbed the shotgun he kept next to the liquor cabinet, cocking it as he reached for the door handle.

"Wait," her mother almost whispered.

"What?" His voice was louder than she wanted it to be, but he wasn't shouting.

"Wait, we don't know who it is. Don't answer it-"

More hammering. The door rattled on its hinges.

"I'm not going to leave it."

"Please," she shifted on her feet, her teeth worrying her bottom lip. "Maybe we could just call someone, or wait for them to go away-"

"Hey," he crossed back over to her, planting a kiss on her forehead. "It's fine. I'm going to handle it, and then we'll get back to this tinsel shit."

She nodded, still visibly unconvinced, watching him walk away from her. He unlatched the door and pulled it open, snapping out a *"yes?"* before he saw who was on the doorstep.

It was his wife. Hair and face and shoulders covered in blood, nightgown shredded, feet bare. Tears in her eyes, deep gashes on her face. Her mouth formed out a *"help"* even though no sound came out.

He froze. His wife in front of him, his wife behind him.

"Who is it?"

He spun, aimed the shotgun at the woman in the living room, fired. The shot rang out, hitting her square in the chest.

"What?" Heather's mother whispered, watching the blood trickle down her chest. She slumped backwards, hitting shelves and leaving blood smears as she hit the floor. "Honey?"

Heather's father turned back to the woman at the door, to the blood on her face, the wild deer pupils of her eyes. The wolf canines of her teeth that didn't quite fit into her mouth.

"Dad?"

Heather in the doorway, swimming in one of his band t-shirts, one sock around her calf and the other around her ankle. Hair tangled from sleep. Her mother was bleeding out in the corner.

"Dad, what's happening?"

He looked at her. Her wide eyes, the soft chub of her cheeks, her trembling lip. He chose.

Heather watched her father aim at the bloodied woman in the doorway and fire. She ran to her room, slammed the door, wiggled out the window. She spent three hours in the dark, stumbling through trees and leaves, sobbing and shivering. The other four were spent in the sheriff's office.

When she found her way back home, half frozen in the early morning, the doorstep was freshly scrubbed and the bookcase was smouldering ash in the driveway. Her father was dead asleep. Her mother was gone. They never spoke of it again.

It was barely light when Heather rolled out of bed, taking a moment to stretch before it was back to business. She'd had a couple of hours of sleep earlier that evening, waking up when her dad slammed the front door shut near midnight. After a few hours of tangling herself further in her sheets, she'd given up on sleep, instead thumbing through the stack of paperbacks she'd acquired months ago and never gotten around to reading. Most of the words didn't sink in, but it was something to do.

She pulled on jeans, a vest, a threadbare shirt, a sweater. In the kitchen, she used a faded letter magnet to tack up an old field trip letter her dad hadn't seen in the first place. She dropped a couple of chocolate bars and a half full bottle of whisky into her backpack, zipped it up, and stepped out the back door.

When she rounded the house Tyler's car was parked at the end of the street, far enough away that she hadn't heard the engine. He had the window rolled down despite the fact that the morning wasn't quite warm yet, and he waved when he saw her. She didn't speed up, her joints still getting used to being upright, and tied her hair up with a scarf that used to be her mother's.

"Hey," Tyler smiled when she was close enough that he didn't have to raise his voice, watching her slide into the passenger seat. "I got you a coffee. It's a long drive."

"Yeah, I know." Heather spent a solitary second attempting to identify why she was annoyed - then she picked up the paper cup, downing as much of the liquid as she could before it burned her. A few hours ago, she had pictured the five hour drive as a series of snapshots, her gazing out of the window, thumbing through one of the paperbacks of short horror she had thrown into her backpack, Tyler switching radio stations while he gazed out longingly into the open road. Now that she was in the annoyingly worn leather of the passenger seat, she realised that was a brief dream. She was in for five hours of mild irritation.

Basil's State Asylum was an imposing white brick structure, stretching up into the hazy summer sky and sprawling over the well-manicured lawn. Green ivy scaled the building, wrapping itself around the iron bars crossed over windows and the grey slates of the roof. The gravel lot in front of the stone steps curved to meet the cobblestone-style fence, from which sprouted metal rods that twisted and warped into barbed wire at the top. Dead leaves littered the doorstep.

Tyler parked the car in front of a wooden stake, topped with a piece of paper that had *visitors* neatly printed on it, gravel crunching under the tires. He turned the engine off, twisting to the passenger seat. Heather had pulled the sleeves of her sweater over her hands, staring blankly at the locks on the front door of the asylum. The book she was reading had slipped closed in her lap, her page unmarked.

"Hey," he tried weakly. "You know, if this is too much-"

"I called ahead, so they should know we're coming," she forced out. "If we just stick to the story, it'll get us in the room, and that will give us the space to ask her questions without anyone overhearing. Probably." Her words were certain, but her voice wavered a little.

"How do you know all this?" Tyler craned forward, peering up the imposing windows and tasteful facade.

Heather snapped out of her memory whirlwind, dropping her book on the dashboard. "How do you think?"

"Oh, I- I didn't mean-"

"It's fine, okay?" Heather pushed open the door. "Let's go do this."

The two of them, Heather feeling awkwardness bubbling up around her, made their way to the chipped front steps. Tyler hesitated at the doorstep, but Heather breezed straight past him, one fist relentlessly knocking on the door.

"Hello?" she called out. Tyler almost audibly rolled his eyes, both impressed and embarrassed.

"Good morning," a woman in her mid-fifties, infinite patience in her tired eyes, cracked open the door to squint at the two of them. Heather cleared her throat and, in a way that made his skin crawl, lies started tumbling out.

"Good morning, we're the niece and nephew of Jane Whivers. We're just here to see our aunt, it's a family tradition that-"

"I heard," the receptionist answered in a short, clipped tone, one that did not broker either facts or nonsense. She paused, and Tyler felt like she could see every bad thing he had ever done written on his face. Heather thought that if she rolled up her sleeves, her medical records would be inked on her forearms.

Instead, she smiled. "Come on in."

The door opened, and she led them down a white limestone hallway scrubbed within an inch of its life. Heather resisted the urge to trail her fingers over the blank, fading wallpaper. They passed a nurse's station, the glass barrier reinforced with metal wire, the opening bolted down. The white wash wooden doors were propped open all down the hall - she guessed whatever after-lunch happy pills were kicking in, and the building would be as quiet as possible. Probably not the best for the interview they were trying to conduct.

"She's in here," the nurse stopped by a door, number 110, a patient's chart hanging on the wall. "Now, she's not always the most receptive, or agreeable, but I reckon you know that."

Heather was nodding before Tyler had a chance to open his mouth.

"I'm just down the hall. Shout if you need help." A professional distance - Heather could respect it, as much as being this side of the hallway made her skin crawl.

"Thanks," she snagged Tyler's sleeve, pulling him inside.

The room was as sun-soaked as the bars outside would allow. There was a plywood dresser across from the door, a map indicating hiking trails - no frame - tacked to the wall, a narrow frame with a thin blue mattress on top of it. On the mattress sat a woman who couldn't have been older than twenty-eight, but her face was pale and sallow, her eyes almost rapid.

"Hey," Heather took a half-step closer, knowing there was an invisible line somewhere in this room she didn't want to cross. "My name's Heather, and this is Tyler. We're from-"

"I don't have any fucking siblings," Jane snapped, her spine straightening. The blanket slid off her shoulders, the muscles in her arms tensing. She hadn't spent the last few years staring at the walls. "So who the fuck are you?"

"We're from Lovely, and we have questions. About the camp," Tyler moved past Heather, deeper into the room that she wanted to. She bit her tongue.

"You think I did it?" Jane's eyes were steel, her mouth a hard line.

"We think some *thing* did it," the usual playfulness in Tyler's voice was gone. "And we think you may have the answers to some of our questions."

Jane scanned the two of them, openly distrusting in a way that Heather admired. "You guys one of them? Come back to finish the job?"

"No! No," Tyler scrambled. "We think people might be in danger. I- I think those things killed my brother."

Heather didn't look at him, couldn't acknowledge the waver in his voice or she would crumble. "I think another person's going to die by the end of the summer."

Jane deliberated for a moment, eyes flicking between the two of them. "Alright. Hit me with the questions."

He faltered here. Tyler had spent the ride up planning on convincing his way into this room, and now that he was here, he was running out of map.

Heather half-smiled. "You want a cigarette?"

Jane stared, eyebrows drawing together. "God, yes."

Tyler watched the two of them trade a pack, a lighter, taking turns. There was an uncomfortable ease in the way Heather leant against the wall, more natural than she'd ever seemed in a school hallway.

"Alright, so," Heather exhaled smoke, her eyes on Jane, "we know there's something out there killing kids, every few years or so. What do we do?"

"Well, step one, don't get yourself hospitalised. Which means no adults, and no sheriff," Jane tapped ash onto her floor. "Definitely no sheriff."

"We figured that much out," Tyler nodded.

"Good," Jane shrugged. "And they change. That's important, you need to remember that. They copy, they mimic, they imitate. One second there's a deer tapping at your window, then it's a vulture, then it's the dead kid you found in a wardrobe years ago, stood upright."

"They- they're here?" Tyler stepped towards the window, squinting in the sunlight.

Jane turned back to Heather. "They remember. If they think you know, if they think they should have you, they'll come after you. Trust me, I know."

"Is that why you're still here?" Heather asked, stubbing out her cigarette on the bottom of her shoe.

Jane winced. "Yeah. That and the fact that I have no idea what I would do if I ever stepped outside again."

"Yeah, I get that feeling."

"I don't-" Jane was looking up at her, her eyes wide. "I don't remember what sunlight feels like. You're so fucked, you know that? You get out, you start running-"

Tyler was taking a step back, his eyes darting to the door. "Heather, maybe we should go-"

"No!" Jane lunged, her hands wrapped around Heather's wrist. "Don't go, please, no one else believes me, they think-"

"Heather, I think-"

"No, Jane, it's-"

Her grip tightened, nails digging in. "They'll get you, they'll fucking get you, you need to run-"

"Heather, I really think-"

"It's too late! They know your face, they know, they know-"

Tyler pulled Heather back, her skin scraping. "Jane, I'm sorry, we should-"

Jane slumped down, elbows on the bed frame, her eyes darkening. A little bit of the fight going out. "Fine, leave. Crawl back to Lovely. Don't come crying to me when one of you is dead in September."

"I'm sorry," Heather forced out, letting Tyler drag her down the hallway. He said something to the nurse she couldn't - wouldn't - hear, helped her into the car. The sunlight burned, the gravel under her feet deafened her. She watched him buckle her seatbelt from the outside, saw him kiss a stranger's cheek. Drying traces of someone else's blood on her sleeves.

Four months ago. The first week of April, the apple trees in Lovely blossoming and litters of rabbits tumbling through well-kept lawns. Heather, what could have been an ocean away.

She was curled up on a mattress that was lumpy whichever way she lay on it, cold under a thin blue blanket and a hospital gown. Her gaze was on the dust swirling in a pale sunbeam, her hands wrapped around herself.

"Lunch."

She pushed herself up, looking at the nurse in the doorway. Penelope, her golden hair braided and her shirt freshly starched, as always. In her hands was a plastic orange tray and a paper cup.

Heather nodded. She took the cup, downed the pills in it - pink tablet, two blue capsules, yellow tablet, she'd forgotten the names - opened her mouth as proof. Penelope nodded, handing her the tray. She would be back in twenty minutes to make sure Heather had eaten it all. If not, more pills, injections, straps tying her to the bed. Fun.

Lunch was a plastic cup of orange juice, a piece of bread, a scoop of mashed potato, grilled chicken strips, sweetcorn. She missed the cooling feeling of glass. She missed silverware. She missed alcohol, choices, Tyler, control, seeing her wrists instead of thick gauze. She chewed, swallowed.

On Sunday - every Sunday - Heather would pull herself out of bed, shower while Penelope watched, sit on cold, wet tile and watch as more gauze was wrapped around her forearms. She would lie in her bed, thumbing through one of the few books that were allowed in the recreation room - nothing too disturbing, god forbid - and wait. The girl across the hall, who had pushed her little brother out of a third floor window while sleepwalking, had visitors every week. The woman four doors down, bald because she had pulled out all of her hair and most of her eyebrows in a moment of sadness, had a visitor once a month. At the far end of the hall, an elderly woman so high up with morphine she walked into a wall once and didn't feel it, would have multiple visits crammed in this one day. Heather couldn't remember the rest, didn't raise her head that many times or have it in her to hold whatever name or circumstance against them, but there were days she was duly surprised the floorboards didn't collapse from how trodden they were. The nurses were her only visitors.

There was a phone in the hallway, a chipped black receiver built into the wall across from the desk where a nurse or doctor always sat. They used to have a yellow pages phonebook, sat on the floor under the phone, until someone threw it against the wall so hard it left a dent. Heather didn't know who did it, except it wasn't her. Some nights she would sit up wondering if it was her. Usually, there would be a line by the phone, snaking down the hall, feet tapping as they waited - except for Mondays, when the urge for a familiar voice was mostly satiated.

Heather spent a lot of Mondays leaning against that wall, dialing the first nine digits of Tyler's phone number, hanging up. Repeat. There were plenty of reasons not to call him - it was his parents' number, he should be in school, what would she even say with a trained professional listening? Her first phone call to her father's answering machine to *please please please please come get me, I'm sorry, I won't do it again I didn't mean to* had earnt her a lavender coloured pill that made her thoughts feel like honey oozing through her fingers for what they told her was four days. Of course, there were many more reasons to call Tyler, the list of which dragged her to that hallway once a week. She spent a lot of Mondays not calling Tyler.

Tuesdays and Thursdays, she would drag herself to the psychiatrist's office, up three spiralling flights of stairs, to sit in a cold wooden chair across from a doctor.

No, she didn't have any thoughts of hurting herself. Yes, she regretted her actions. Yes, she knew better now. No, she wasn't resisting treatment. No, she wasn't lying. Yes, she just wanted to go home let me go home let me go home let me out let me-

She would stare out of the recreational room windows, watching flowers bloom and the grass get mowed, chewing her nails. Sometimes, she wondered if the outside world had already forgotten her. She waited.

And then, a new tax year and brand shiny new pay cuts and Heather, like so many other patients not quite exciting enough for a doctor to vouch for her, was chewed up and spit back out. Overnight, her clothes were returned to her and the cups of forget-me-not blue pills taken away and there she was, on the cement curb outside the hospital, shivering in the wind. A taxi pulling up. One long drive to remember who she was and what, if anything, she wanted. The slow march back to Lovely.

Tyler let the engine idle for a moment, before switching it off. They were in the road next to Heather's house, the street dark other than the sparse lampposts. For a second, Heather let herself pretend that he was dropping her off after a second date, that he would step out of the car to open her door, wait in the driveway to make sure she made it up the garden path. That the weight of the world wasn't pressing down on her shoulders.

"You know, I could come inside," Tyler tried weakly. "If you need me to talk to your dad."

"I don't want your folks to worry." There was a light on in the living room, but nowhere else in the house. Unspecific. "I have it handled."

"If you say so." He ran his thumb over her knuckles, only adding to the brief fantasy she was entertaining. "You know, if you ever need somewhere to stay-"

"I know," she pushed the door open, grabbing her backpack.

"Do you really think someone else is going to die this summer?"

She turned back to him, watching the shadows dance on his face. She didn't like lying to him like this. "I don't know, honestly. I don't think so. I'll see you tomorrow, alright?"

"Alright."

He was gone before she made it halfway over the lawn. The front door was unlocked, and she closed it whisper-silently behind her. Her hand hovered over the latch, deliberating which opinion would be safer.

"So that's where you've been sneaking off to."

Heather spun, and her father was there, shadowing the doorway to the kitchen. There was a half-empty bottle of liquor in his hand, and she could smell his breath from where she was.

"Dad, I don't know what you're-"

"You think I don't notice?" His voice was getting louder, his frame swaying. "You're sneaking out, you're not home most nights, you're not at school either. You're stealing my fucking alcohol to what, make that boy keep you around?"

"It's not like that-"

"You're a stupid kid, you know that? You're going to drop out of school, after everything I've done for you, and what do you think is going to happen? That Henderson boy is never going to marry you, his father will make sure of it. What happens when the fucking hangover hits, huh? You're going to make exactly the same mistakes your mother made-"

"The only mistake Mum made was marrying you," Heather snapped. She didn't realise how much she meant it until the words were out of her mouth.

The rage in her father's eyes hit her before the bottle almost did, shattering against the doorframe and spraying her with liquid and shards of glass. He lunged for her and she bolted for the corner, trying to get the coffee table between them. Her father hit the door, hard, and she sprinted into the dark kitchen, hitting her hip on the doorknob. He slammed into her, sending her into the countertop. He wrenched a kitchen drawer open, fumbling for a knife as she pried open the latch on the backdoor.

"You go out there, you don't come back," he snarled. The moonlight shone on a steak knife in his hand. Something howled in the woods behind her. "And if I see you again, I'll fucking kill you."

Heather hated to admit it, but she faltered for just a moment, one foot out of the door. Then he took a staggering step towards her and she ran, lungs burning, legs sore, tree branches scraping at her face. Kept running, until the yellow kitchen light was behind her.

Heather's dad stood in the doorway, watching his daughter vanish into the dark woods. He stood there, listening to the howls coming from the woods, the distant sirens blaring. He waited until he was sure she wasn't coming back, and then he deadbolted both the front and back doors, and made sure the rifle by his bed was fully loaded. He placed the photograph of the three of them, a snapshot of a happy family on Heather's first birthday, that lived on his bedside table, face down.

It is nighttime. It is nighttime, and Heather is in the woods, by herself. She knows what lies in the forest - it may know she's there too.

Heather made it to the liquor store before her adrenaline started faltering and the lack of air reached her. The heat of the night beat down on her; it was getting hotter, summer rapidly approaching, the warm breath of the forest making it harder to pant. She turned in a slow circle, trying to catch any sign of movement. Heartbeat in her ears. The branches weren't swaying in the wind, and she couldn't see any animals. There was another howl, and it may have just been her mind playing tricks on her, but it sounded closer this time. She couldn't stay here.

What Heather didn't know, but could just about sense, was that it was not the branches that moved at night. Instead, the branches stayed perfectly still, hundreds of hundreds of branches replicating the exact same position. By extending the limbs, the trees moved, whole root structures shifting and rearranging in a way imperceptible to the human eye - especially a paranoid and exhausted human eye.

The liquor store was closed - she could see that from the treeline, not that midnight is a particularly busy time for any part of Lovely. The glare of the lights mounted on the walls of the store illuminated the road and car park around itself, creating an almost silver glow against the dark of the woods. If she stepped forward, she would be bathed in that artificial halo, a spotlit target. Not that she felt any safer in the woods.

Where the fuck do I go? Her house was no longer an option. Tyler lived on the other side of whatever was in the woods. She thought of the newspaper article she'd read in his car earlier today, of a teenage girl found strung up in the trees, the bones of her arms and legs pulled out of their sockets, moss already growing around her body when they found her. Heather started walking.

She was by far the loudest thing in the forest that night. Twigs snapped under her footsteps, her backpack snagged on a bush, her heart was beating so loudly it threatened to shake the trees. Heather wasn't just easy to track, she was impossible not to. A squirrel above her stopped chewing on a tree branch to watch her. A vulture with human eyes let out a low squawk. A coyote, dried blood on its muzzle, raised its head and sniffed. She kept walking, and then she started running again.

The woods followed her. It was less of an elegant trap, or a strategic consequence of her prodding and probing at the history and very ecosystem of Lovely - it was closer to the fact that she was a moving target, and nothing more exciting was happening at that moment.

Heather sprinted over the tangled roots and dirt floor, certain something was following her, too scared to turn around to look. She skidded down a bank, the moon lighting the way. There were heavy footsteps behind her - a deer, catching up, mouth frothing at the idea of tearing into soft flesh. A shadow passed above her, an owl giving up hunting a mouse for more enticing prey. Slithering through the undergrowth, a rattlesnake passed mere feet from her, ready to trip her if nothing else did. Heather kept running, tasting blood, ripping free of the tree line and onto the asphalt car park in front of the sheriff's office, lit up like a lighthouse in the storm.

The deer stopped running, staying in the shadows of the woods, hooves stomping in frustration. The owl alighted onto a branch, cocking its head in a way more suited to dogs. Just outside of the light cast onto the forest, animals stopped their pursuit, staring at Heather, watching her barrel into the sheriff's office and slam the door behind her. She spun to stare at the dark outside, heaving gasps of air, frantically searching the night for any sign of movement, of danger. It was still out there, too still. The woods waited.

In a half-asleep stupor, the twenty seconds between waking and fully gaining consciousness, Tyler groped a hand through his bed, searching for Heather's body. His fingers pulled at cold sheets and he blinked, squinting at the lamp still lit on his desk. It was still dark outside, night, and his phone was ringing.

Tyler rolled out of bed, stumbling upright and picking up the phone.

"Hello?" he croaked, rubbing at his eyes.

"Tyler?" It was Heather, her voice sounding panicked.

"What time is it?"

"Can you come and get me? Please?"

"What are you talking about?" he fumbled his watch out of the drawer in his desk, which ticked out 1:03 a.m.

"I'm at the sheriff's office."

His heart dropped. He was awake now, no longer sifting through his belongings. "What?"

"Just come get me, okay?" The line went dead.

Two minutes later and he was behind the wheel, the belt in his jeans unbuckled, shirt wrinkled with sleep, his father's shotgun in the backpack next to him. He pushed his car as fast as it could go, faster than he had during races with his friends, faster than when he had to identify Max's body, bloated and bloodless, fresh from the lake. He was at the police station less than twenty minutes after Heather called, burning rubber and slamming on the breaks.

Other than one light over the entrance door to the station, it was lost into darkness, every bulb inside put out. His headlights shone yellow beams onto the windows, not betraying any movement inside. It could be a trap, could be some *thing* using Heather's voice, twisting her vocal cords, luring him out to the edge of town in the dead of night, alone. It could be, and she could be miles away, safe and sound. Tyler climbed out of the car and slammed open the station door, screaming her name.

The sheriff's office sat in a half-asleep silence, blackness filling the waiting room. Tyler wished he had brought a torch with him, or a sledgehammer. He unzipped the backpack on his arm, fumbling inside it, trying to angle the porch light to his advantage. There must have been a light switch near him. His hand curled around the metal of a barrel, just as the low hum of a generator started back up and the room flooded with weak fluorescents.

The waiting room looked like a crime scene, if he allowed so much irony in this moment. Chairs were strewn over, blood drying on the carpet and the walls, a potted plant smashed to pieces. Missing posters ripped down, the door to the still-dark office propped open, the public phone hanging taunt on its cord. The hallway leading out of the room stretched out into nothing. Tyler hesitated, and then took a deep breath.

"Heather?"

A sound, from beyond this room. He didn't want to point a shotgun at his friend; he didn't want to leave himself defenceless. Tyler waited.

The door to the office creaked open, sent shivers down his spine, and then Heather was there. Heather, blood staining her cheek, sweater ripped open, but upright and walking. His hand loosened, the backpack almost sliding off his shoulder.

"Heather? I came as soon as I could, I-"

"Shut up and get in here." Her voice was tense, angry. He couldn't read the look on her face.

Tyler slid inside the office, aware the relief he was feeling was short-lived. Heather slammed the door behind him, forcing a heavy oak desk in front of it.

"It's really you, right?" she snapped, her hand reaching around to her back pocket.

"What? Yes, it's me. Relax." He tried to chuckle, found himself coming up short.

"How did we meet? The first time?" Her eyes were cold, almost feeling, every wall she had built was put up.

"Um, alright," the room behind her was still in shadow, barely any light streaming through the shutters on the glass panelling. "We were younger, maybe twelve?" He registered the look on her face. "Definitely twelve. You came to one of my birthday parties and didn't talk to anyone, and then I tracked you down to the kitchen to give you a cupcake. It was buttercream with blue sprinkles, the same colour as your dress. And I told you to come by anytime, and gave you our phone number, and you didn't even smile," he faltered. "I think about that all the time."

Heather nodded. "Okay, it's you." She pushed the desk harder against the door and then, finally allowing the look on his face, shot him a distracted smile.

"Heather? What's going on?" Tyler wrapped a hand around her arm, and was honestly more disturbed when she didn't pull away, his fingers sliding under the woolen tatters and gripping skin.

"The sheriff is a mimic, or whatever we're calling them." Her voice was serious, her gaze trained on the slats of the shutters. "So was the deputy. We can hurt them, kill them even, but we have to be smart about it. We're not safe here."

"Okay," Tyler nodded, in a way that a person that has realised that only one thing matters to them does. "Where do we go?"

"Not your house, or mine." She pulled the handgun out of her waistband, turned off the safety. "Armory is our best bet, I think, until morning."

"What happens in the morning?" He asked, and she shrugged.

Heather grabbed his hand, pulling him through the darkness of the office. She slid open a door disguised as wooden panels, led him through twists and turns illuminated by weak light bulbs. Tyler stumbled into exposed wires, jutting pipes, almost hit his head ducking out of the wall space they were in and into a brightly lit room. The walls were adorned with weapons, shotguns and crossbows and blades covering every inch but one air vent, and there was a metal table in the centre of the room.

"Help me with this?" Heather half-asked, half-instructed, dropping her backpack and placing her gun on top of it. Tyler dropped his stuff down, grabbing one side of the table and manoeuvring it flush against the door. She slumped down against the opposite wall, wrapping her arms around her legs, eyes glued to the hinges. Tyler waited for a moment, then sat down next to her.

"What happened?" he asked, resisting the urge to wrap his arm around her. He knew better than to push his luck.

"My dad kicked me out, and I was just in the woods and it felt wrong. And I started running, and I ended up here, and the sheriff was here. And the deputy. They know, Tyler. They know." She leant her head back, dirt streaking her face. Her hand was tensed around the gun again.

"Are you okay?"

"I killed the deputy."

His breath caught. For a moment, he wondered if it was safer on the other side of that door. "What?"

"Yeah," she rubbed her eyes with her left hand, fast. It struck Tyler how, under bright lights and with her guard crumbling, she looked younger than she was. Weaker. "I got him by surprise. He tried to change, his skin went scaly and his hands looked like an alligator's claws. Somehow it was too late, I didn't," she squeezed her eyes closed, "I don't know what I'm doing."

He did touch her this time, his knuckles brushing against her cheek. "Are you hurt?"

She shook her head. "Not badly. Sheriff shredded my fucking sweater, but it's just a few scrapes and bruises. I'm alright."

"Good." Tyler nodded, shifting closer to her. "So we wait here until morning, then we figure it out from there?"

"Yeah, I think so. I don't think we should be out after dark," she chuckled, humourlessly. She sounded like every teacher and parent she'd ever made fun of. The joke was not lost on either of them.

He smiled at her, really hoping it would come off as genuine. "Okay, that sounds like a plan. We'll be alright." He hoped the reassurance in his voice would help, even if she stayed slumped on the floor. "In the meantime... do you have any alcohol on you?"

Heather laughed, with actual humour in her voice this time. "Do you think they'll let me smoke in here?"

Four miles away from the sheriff's office was Lovely's main telephone mast, the town's bridge to the outside world. There was a police car parked a few hundred feet from it, the door left open and the red-blue lights still flickering on. Silhouetted in front of the mast was the sheriff, an axe in his hands, the wood slotting into the callouses that he didn't want to heal. He lifted the axe above his head, and swung.

The payphones - outside Tyler's work, the diner, on Main Street, by the school - all blared out a quick s.o.s.. No one else noticed it - but if they did, they brushed it off as just one of those things. But, deep in her heart, heather knew all other hope was lost.

In the body of a hare, something sat in the gutter opposite Mr Strand's house, beady eyes tracked on the front door. The lights were burning up the energy bill in the living room despite the entire house being still, and no one had been in or out. If someone were to try the back garden, the vulture perched on a tree branch would see them. The sheriff swung his axe again.

Outside the Henderson's house, a small herd of deer were weaving through the trees. They paced through the back garden, nibbling on shrubs and rhododendron flowers, their Tyler-grey eyes never straying from the house. One of the fawns picked a circle to the front garden, curling up neatly underneath the mailbox, a line of spittle falling from its gleaming canines. His mother, having stumbled downstairs and promptly fallen unconscious on the living room sofa, was squarely in its line of sight. The axe bit the tree again.

At the lake, an alligator slithered through the murky depths, nostrils above the surface. Its webbed feet reached the silk mud of the bank and an elk pulled itself out of the water, fur damp, antlers reaching up into the night sky. It crossed into the tree line, another of the many uncharacteristically restless animals in the woods that night. If a wildlife expert had taken a stroll in Lovely that night, they would have had questions - but there were none asked, not that night.

The sheriff swung again, and the telephone mast fell.

According to the brass hands of a wristwatch Tyler had found in the front pocket of his backpack, the accuracy of which was questionable, it had been three hours, placing them at roughly four a.m. Heather had finally stretched out her legs and made a considerable effort to unclench her shoulders, while Tyler was sitting cross-legged next to her, his arm between her spine and the wall. They were passing back and forth a whisky bottle, now almost empty, found to neither of their surprise in Heather's bag.

"-so I'm standing in his office, right, freaking out," Heather was saying. Tyler had one hand over his mouth, trying not to drown her out with his laughter. "And he's all, 'what are you doing here?' and 'if you have an official inquiry, you'll have to return in the morning', and I've got one foot out the door, and-"

"You did not-"

"And the deputy walks in, and I just shoot him."

Tyler's mouth gaped open, a stunned laugh falling from his lips. "You shot him?"

Heather nodded, taking a gulp of liquor. "I honestly don't know which of us were more surprised. Anyway, so I shoot him, he's bleeding out on the office carpet, the sheriff is yelling, I am panicking, and then the sheriff morphs into a bat and the next thing I know, the lights are out and there's some*thing* scratching me. I hit it, pretty hard-"

"*Pretty* hard?"

"-and it sends me flying into the wall, which gives way into the tunnel, and then I end up here."

Tyler paused, drank, and turned back to her. "That is the most insane story I have ever heard."

"No, I know," she laughed.

"I am so serious. I would have shit myself if that was me," Tyler laughed. Heather's eyes darted up, suddenly feeling like she was missing out on something. "I cannot believe you killed the-"

"Wait, shut up," Heather clamped a hand over his mouth, tensing up. Other hand back on the gun.

"What was that sound?"

Tyler twisted to peer at the door, over the block of the table, trying to stay low. "I don't-"

"What the fuck was that sound?"

She heard it again, a small metal grating, like a screw being tightened. It almost hurt to look.

"Don't tell me it's coming from the vent-"

It was - the precise sound Heather had heard was the noise of the four small screws that secured the metal grate to the narrow tunnel of the air conditioning system slowly but steadily being loosened from the inside. This mystery was solved when the vent grate came crashing down, mere inches from Tyler's bent knee, and a swarm of bats tumbled out.

Heather scrambled to her feet before Tyler had a chance to react, firing into the storm cloud of flapping leather. A few of them hit the ground around him with meaty thumps - he watched them twitch there for a moment until they stilled. One of the bats flapped into the wall, trading wings for scales, turning inside out and into a lizard that scuttled down the wall. Heather fired, missed, fired again, her bullet nailing it to the ground. He looked away as its bones crunched under her boot.

"You okay?" Heather asked him, almost snapping, as she pulled a handgun off the wall and checked the bullet chamber. He didn't take it personally.

"Yeah, I'm good," he forced a smile. She turned around, gun drawn, and saw two identical Tylers gazing back up at her.

༄

Three years ago, the summer when they were both fourteen, Tyler's parents were out of town for the weekend on a business trip turned anniversary getaway. It wasn't the hugest news, nothing that would make the papers or even alert any parents, but it made enough of a buzz that every kid in their year knew he was left without a babysitter. Tyler didn't often cave to social pressure, but he had picked the lock on the liquor cabinet, and he was throwing a party - Max had already been bribed with more chocolate than any ten year old could have asked for, and he would have all of Sunday to clean up the evidence. The perfect plan.

Heather's dad had been working longer hours that summer, begrudgingly giving her a house key and a few dollars a week for necessities. He would leave before nine, stumble in drunk well after dark, spend the weekends sprawled on the sofa in front of mindless reruns, working on a to-go order and a six pack of cheap beer. The two of them cordially avoided each other, leaving Heather staring at the walls of her room more often than she would have liked.

That Friday, bored out of her mind with the same twelve paperbacks, she made her routine walk into town, scouring the streets for an adventure, or at least a distraction. The money her dad left her wasn't quite enough for an order of the pastel-coloured ice creams the girls in her class would giggle over, but it would let her wander through the grocery store and maybe pick out some gum, if she didn't browse for long enough to annoy the shop clerk. She was there, leafing through glossy magazines with a forced absentmindedness, when Bethany and her friends walked in. Heather hid in the frozen aisle.

"-he's *so* lucky!"

"I know, I wish my parents were that cool. Apparently there are going to be seniors there."

"There are not!"

"Well, Peter said-"

"Oh hey, Heather."

Heather looked up from pretending to browse frozen pancakes boxes to see Bethany, clad in a gingham sundress, shaded glasses on top of her curled pigtails, holding two scoops of pink ice cream with the grace of a champagne flute, at the end of the aisle. Annie and Matilda stood behind her, ice cream in hands, both fallen silent.

"Hey," Heather forced out, trying to make her smile seem friendly. She was suddenly very aware of her faded jeans and slightly stained checkered shirt, and the fact that she may be blushing.

"You… shopping?" Bethany asked, tilting her head. There was nothing particularly mocking in her tone, but the look Annie and Matilda exchanged was more than enough.

"Um, yeah. My dad-"

"Okay, don't let us distract you."

A month ago, Heather had found a mouse in one of the traps her dad set up on the front step, still alive. She had carried it a half mile into the woods, setting its stunned body on a mossy patch of roots and tucking a flower beside it. They would have something in common now, she thought, if they ever met again.

Bethany shot her a smile that was almost dazzling, turning to leave. Heather bit her lip, trying not to hold her breath.

"Oh, before you go," Bethany looked over her shoulder, in a move Heather would have bet the few dollars she had was practised. "Are you going to Tyler's party tomorrow night? It's supposed to be *insane*."

Heather thought she was going to be sick. "Um, I'm not sure. It depends if my dad can give me a ride back or-"

"Okay," Bethany's smile never wavered, but Annie was snickering next to her. "Well, I hope I see you there, Heather."

They walked away then, leaving Heather shivering in the store. Her cheeks were red, she knew that much. She was too old to cry about this kind of stuff.

Heather spent the rest of the day in her bed, blankets pulled over her head, hugging a pillow. It was moments like this that she wished she could pick up the phone and tell someone about those *bitches*. She didn't want it to bother her. She didn't want to feel like she had to go to that party.

It was past six on Saturday when she next left her room, tip-toeing down the hall and into the living room. Her dad, as predicted, was passed out on the sofa, head leant back, television blasting a sitcom. There was a half-drunk bottle of whisky on the coffee table next to his slippered feet and empty plate. Heather padded towards him, eyes trained on the rise and fall of his stomach, switching out the bottle with an empty one she had been using as a vase. In the liquor cabinet, she traded the half-empty bottle for a full one, before heading back to her room. She was going to that party.

Ten minutes later and she was walking to the Henderson's house in a clean pair of jeans, polished boots, vaguely flattering blue shirt on. Her hair was held in a ponytail by one of her mum's old ribbons, and her school bag was over her shoulder, carrying liquor and a pack of cigarettes she had just started enjoying smoking.

Tyler's lawn was already full of teenagers when she got there. Music was blasting through the open windows, a couple was making out in a car parked on the drive, some kid was chugging a beer while a group cheered him on. Heather hesitated, stood by the mailbox, painfully sober. She paused, then pulled open the backpack and took a burning gulp.

"Wow, that's a strong drink."

She turned, half-lowering the bottle, and saw Tyler stood beside her, smiling. She had to look up at him, his glowing grey eyes and golden hair, dressed in a crisp shirt and expensive-looking jeans. Logically, she knew they were roughly the same age, but he carried himself with an amount of confidence most fourteen-year-olds didn't.

"I mean, I would ask what you were drinking, but-"

"Do you want some?" she was speaking before she knew she was. Her hand held out the bottle, straight liquor, to Tyler. He looked at her, let the sentence hang in the air long enough for her to almost squirm.

"Sure," he said, taking it from her. Tyler took a sip, still holding eye contact, before sputtering out a cough, clamping one hand over his mouth as he tried to choke it down. Heather laughed. He grinned at her.

"Here," he passed the bottle back to her. "I may need something weaker. There's beer in the kitchen."

She took a step back. "Okay, I can-"

"Come with me." He brushed his hand over her shoulder, before striding up the lawn. Heather followed.

The rest of the night was a blur of smoke breaks and hard liquor. Tyler circled through the crowd, life of the party, sipping beers and making jokes. Heather hugged the kitchen counter he'd leant her against, wondering how early she could leave before it would make her look rude. No one tried to talk to her, which was the way she liked it.

Eleven p.m. hit and, as the first of the parents started arriving outside, she slipped out of the back door. Heather leant against the back of the house, taking another long gulp to give her enough courage to walk home. The door opened, spilling light into the garden, and she flinched away on instinct.

"Heather? Hey, you leaving already?" Tyler, stumbling outside, hair in his eyes.

"Um, yeah," she half-smiled. "It's getting late, and I don't think this is really my crowd-"

"You had a good time though, right?" He stood next to her, swaying slightly, one hand on the wall.

"Yeah, I had a good time." She took another sip.

"Okay, I'm glad. Look, a lot of people are leaving so I get if it's time to go but if you want to stay, I-"

"Oh, I don't-"

"I'm glad you came." His hand was on her shoulder, the second time that night.

"Thank you. And, you know, thank you for having me."

He beamed, honestly beamed. "Any time."

Heather faltered, thought about her father drunkenly sleeping on the sofa. Banished that thought. "You know, I think I could stay for another drink."

His face made it worth it.

That summer, Heather went over to Tyler's house twelve more times, always when his parents were away or fast asleep. He called her seven times when she was home alone. Once, he bought her a cheap stuffed rabbit toy and left it in her bag for her to find later.

School started again that autumn, and they didn't talk in the hallways. They didn't sit next to each other in class, or have lunch together. But he was the first person to wish her a happy birthday, and she was the first person to sit shotgun in his new car. As far as either of them were concerned, they were the best of friends.

For the first time that night, staring at the two Tylers, Heather froze. *Think think think think.* Two Tylers, both staring up at her with those daydream fuelling eyes, identical forced smiles on their dimpled faces. Her breath caught, her hands tightening on the gun. There were no more bats to shoot.

The Tylers saw each other, flinched as Tyler would, stumbled to their feet. Two voices insisted it was him, that she knew it was him, who else could it be?

"Heather, c'mon, it's me-"

"Heather, you know I would never-"

"Please, it's Tyler-"

"Please, I'm your friend-"

"Remember my twelfth birthday-"

"Remember my twelfth birthday-"

"Shut up," Heather snapped, barrel spinning from one Tyler to the next. "Tell me, um."

The two of them stared back at her, eternally patient, waiting for her next question. His face, waiting for her to lead, make the next move, to jump so he could follow.

"Tell me how you feel about me."

The two Tylers traded glances, just for a moment, just long enough to make her stomach drop.

Tyler on the left turned to her, his gaze almost earnest. "Heather, please. You know it's me, it's *me,* I love you-"

She didn't mean to laugh. The real Tyler - her Tyler - would never. She raised her gun, and she shot him.

The bullet hit him squarely in the chest. Tyler looked down, watching the red stain spreading across his chest as if it was happening to somebody else. He looked up at Heather, the other end of the gun, his hands shaking.

"Heather?" he asked, before crumpling to the ground.

She turned, and the other Tyler's eyes were the orange circles of an owl. He blinked, and they were the wide, brown eyes of a deer. He blinked again, and then they were the eyes of a lizard, a rabbit, a wolf, a vulture, a person again. Heather looked into her own eyes, in not-Tyler's face. She fired, and she screamed.

Not-Tyler shouldered the first bullet, took the next three to the chest, without breaking eye contact. The fourth finally grazed his aorta, spilling enough blood into his chest cavity that he couldn't think straight, too panicked to remember which animal can withstand losing two pints of blood, and the spiralling of his heartbeat only churned out more blood until he was face down, pulse fluttering and fading.

Heather dropped the gun, staggering, falling over to her Tyler. She pulled his head into her lap, cradling, watching the blood bubble from his lips, her fingers slipping over the single bullet wound that was enough to pull the sun from the sky.

No. no, no, no.

He blinked up at her. The corners of his mouth curled up into a sweet, brilliant smile. He was gone.

The deer in the woods, watching the sheriff's office with the slitted eyes of an alligator, heard the howling sob Heather let out. It perked its ears towards the sound, almost horse-like, then went back to chewing the human forearm at its feet.

∽

The sheriff, axe slung over his shoulders, was wandering through the forest, whistling lowly. He wasn't in any hurry - he was the man in charge, after all. Anything that didn't get accomplished in the night would be dealt with in the morning, and so the cycle continued on and on. He was old, you see, very old - far too old to be hurried by the affairs of a few teenagers. Maybe not soon, but he would get to it, and when he did, it would be handled. He was a little too used to the way things were. He would never be ready for change.

Heather, on the other hand, was sprinting through the trees, away from the station. She knew that two miles ahead of her were the town limits of Lovely, and some small part still clung to it being the beginning of the rest of the world. Shotgun in hand, she kept running.

In the barely moonlit dark, she stumbled on to the chipped wooden sign, almost crashing straight into it. The fading black paint spelled out *Lovely - The Safest Town You'll See!*. If she wasn't crying, she would have laughed.

She staggered past it, her breath coming in short gasps, her feet hitting the asphalt of the road. Up the road, north, the only way to go. One foot in front of the other, and then a pair of headlights rounding the bend. She raised a hand to shadow her eyes, her arm moving sluggishly, eyes burning. There was blood on her shirt.

The car stopped in front of her, lights on the trees. She watched the forest, hearing the driver's door swing open and shoes step out.

"Heather?"

Her head snapped around. Mr Henderson. In his work suit, his dark tie loosened, shadows under his eyes, the faint smell of brandy. He'd already buried one son at the start of the summer.

Say something.

"What are you doing out here?" his voice was a forced politeness, an obligatory care. He wasn't quite smiling. "Do you need a ride?"

"No- no, I'm okay, I just-" Finally, some words.

"Is that blood?" She could hear the concern spiking in his voice. "Are you hurt?"

"No! No, I'm fine, this is just-"

"Wait, is my son with you?" He stepped towards her, his hand reaching for her elbow.

He's out pretty late.

"Heather, have you seen my son my son my son my-"

The hand closing around her arm had talons, his voice a stuck record as the thing that wasn't Tyler's dad grabbed her with what was a hand moments ago. She wrenched back, her sweater sleeve shredding, and pulled the shotgun up to face him.

"Don't move."

The thing furrowed its brows, pulling the talon-hand back. "Clever."

"What do you want with me? What's happening in this town?" *How do I stop him from changing?*

It leaned back against the frame of the car, painfully casual. As if this was really her friend's dad, and they were discussing a trivial matter that didn't include loaded guns. "No one knows you're out here, do they?"

All at once, the night felt a lot colder. "Where's the sheriff right now?"

It smiled with only the right side of its mouth, a quirk Mr Henderson had her whole life. Once, she heard two mothers gossiping, swooning, over that smirk. A perfect copy. *Was this its first time being Tyler's dad?*

"What is your plan here, exactly?" it scoffed, slowly untying its tie and unbuttoning its jacket sleeves. "Wander through the woods until someone comes and saves you?"

Heather squared her shoulders. "I'm going to kill the sheriff."

The bullet hit him right between the eyes.

Heather watched the body crumble and hit the ground with baited breath, a part of her still waiting for the flesh to coil and spiral into something else, some other monster gunning for her throat. She almost missed the days when the worst thing was a blank test sheet and a lonely morning. Almost.

She kicked the thing that wasn't Tyler's dad aside, sliding into the driver's seat and starting up the engine. Her foot down on the gas and a hard right turn bit through gravel and landed her on the road going north, away from Lovely. The car breezed on, the speedometer hugging seventy, her knuckles white on the steering wheel. She forced herself to take a deep breath, headlights lighting up the night, suddenly grateful for the four driving lessons the school had forced her to take. The shotgun was nestled into the passenger seat, a comforting glimpse out of the corner of her eye. Mr Henderson's tire tracks reached twenty miles away from the town limits and were rewarded with barbed wire snaked across the asphalt of the road. Heather only managed a gasp as the car flipped over, tires shredded, landing upside down on the slanted dirt side of the road, her body curled in smashed glass on the dashboard. She hit her head on the roof, hard.

The radio clicked on, somehow, the crackled sounds of a pop song playing through the speakers. The same pop song Tyler wouldn't admit he knew all the words to. Heather groaned, shaking glass out of her hair. Her hands bit through shards as she pulled her way out of the jagged remains of the window, fingers still digging into the barrel of her shotgun. In a voice that she hated, she gasped, staggering to her feet as blood trickled down her fingers. Her head hurt. There was a cramp in her neck, glass was clinging to her skin, her shoulders damp. She could feel the tears welling up in her eyes, and she couldn't have guessed which injury prompted it. A hollow pain in her chest. Heather looked down, half expecting to see a tree branch or car headrest poking out through a hole in her ribcage. No such luck.

As she forced her way back up to the road, one stumble after the uphill other, shallow breaths, the car behind her hissed out a last, diesel-tinged breath. It burst into flames, amber licking up the dark metal frame, oil sputtering out and igniting. The fire burnt crimson against the night, the rubber seatbelts squeaking and popping, the wrappers in the passenger seat crumbling into ash. Heather forced herself to look away, the acrid smoke stinging her eyes and spilling fresh tears down her cheeks. She bit her lip, hard, and yanked a glass sliver out of her palm, wincing as she spilled her own fresh blood. Red drops scattered the ground at her feet. She kicked dirt over it, blotting her hand with what was left of the sleeve of her sweater. Butt of the shotgun in her arm, she staggered back onto the road, still heading north. Yes, being on foot would take a lot longer - but nothing took as long as staying still. She kept walking.

Up ahead, just outside a gas station that had been closed and ransacked, metal shutters dented, for as long as she could remember, stood a payphone. A street light shone a plastic sunbeam onto it, crying out like an angel. She increased her speed, actually *ran*, stumbling into the phonebooth. Her fingers smeared blood over the keypad.

"Hello? Hi, I'm outside Lovely and I need help, the sheriff is-"
No dial tone.
She slammed the receiver against its handle, cramming against her ear again. No dial tone. The lights were lighting up. Nothing coming from the speakers.

Heather let the phone slip through her fingers, hanging itself on the cord. She clamped both hands over her mouth, her screams muffled into the night. Her feet kept walking.

She had made it one and a half miles, if the moonlight and the stone road markers older than the town weren't lying to her, before she registered the swift, almost silent footsteps behind her, stepping at the very same time she moved forwards, only making a mistake when her resolve faltered and she took a little longer to put her foot down. Something was following her. Heather was only expecting one thing.

She kept walking, her steps almost even, every part of her trying to keep her breath steady. *Just keep moving. Keep moving until-* the, when you're waiting for it, the unmistakable sound of a heavy boot on dirt streaked asphalt, two footsteps in an almost perfect lockstep with yours. The loudest sound in a muffled forest.

Heather spun, throwing down her backpack, shotgun draw, the movement blurring her vision and sending shooting pain up her spine. The barrel stared down the sheriff, his feet on the road, an axe held ready in his arms. His face didn't betray any hint of surprise, but her eyes trained on his arms watched the veins in his forearm pop. He wasn't ready. Good.

"What is this?" she called out, shoulders tensing. "What the fuck do you want with me?"

The sheriff smiled, a forced, reptilian movement. "Hey, kid," he smiled too wide, a movement that should have cramped the muscles in his cheeks. She could see his molars. "Why don't you put the gun down and roll over?"

Heather grit her teeth, ready for him to take a step closer. To her dismay, she still had the echoes of a conscience - he still looked a little too close to human. "Why Tyler? I don't care about anyone else, just- why him? What did Tyler ever do to you?"

"Oh, Tyler?" he tilted his head in an overly practised movement, one that made her skin crawl. "Oh, I think he was just in the wrong place. His brother too - cute kid, you know. I mean, I guess you would, if anyone. Great kid, real shame what happened to that *child-*"

Her first bullet ripped through his chest, forcing straight through and into the tree trunk behind him. Heather watched the blood trickle out of the gaping wound, then cease, her eyes flicking up the sheriff's still-held grin. He was fine.

Her next bullet struck between his eyes - one blue and the other coyote brown, if she had been close enough to see in the moonlight - and she watched the inky dark blood gush from the head wound. Without meaning to, she counted *one. two. three* - the bleeding stopped. The gap in his forehead ran dry. Heather paused, unsure whether to fire again. She didn't want to waste a bullet if it wouldn't mean anything. She also wasn't going to try to talk herself out of firing another shot, for accuracy's sake.

"If you want target practice, this hardly seems like the time," he flipped the axe over in his hands, making it look feather light. "I mean, it worked on the last few of us you murdered, so I understand. Worked on Tyler too, huh?"

Heather shook her head, lowering the shotgun. Her arms were trembling. "Don't fucking talk about him."

He laughed. "You're cute. I'd say it's a shame it's ending like this, but it's not."

The sheriff swung, axe raising high over his head, silver blade winking in the moonlight. She lurched back, the axe slicing strands of her hair. He moved closer, swinging again, blade biting into the side of her bicep. Heather cried out, blood spilling down her arm, before rapping the butt of the shotgun over his knuckles. His grip loosened, reflexively, just for a moment - long enough for her to drop the shotgun and snatch the axe out of his hands. The sheriff's eyes met hers, and a ripple of scales trickled down under his skin.

The wooden handle was heavy in her hands, sending fresh pain through her already worn thin muscles. She tightened her grip, and swung.

Heather had been aiming for his neck, the strip of skin above his collarbone where a vein should be. The weight of the axe dragged her aim down, the blade slashing through the bullet hole in his chest, spilling fresh blood. She wrenched the axe back, it twisting out and splitting skin. Another swing - crushing through his kneecap, making him buckle, blood splattering the two of them. The sheriff let out a cry, half-howl and half-screech, before throwing himself at her. The two of them hit the ground, the first fallen leaves of the summer crunching underneath her, the wind knocked out of her lungs. Hot blood spilling onto her where the sheriff's shoulder met the axe. She took a ragged, gasping breath, his face inches from hers, too many teeth for him to shut his mouth. His hands wrapped around her throat, squeezing down on her windpipe. The edges of her vision started to go dark. It hurt.

Heather tried to take a deep breath, found that she couldn't. Her hands tightened on the axe. She tensed her shoulders before shoving the axe upwards, cleaving it towards the sky. The pressure on her throat loosened.

There was a soft *thud* to her left as the sheriff's severed arm hit the ground beside her, dirt flicking onto her cheek. He screamed, a sound that was almost human except for how high-pitched it was. Heather rolled out from under him, the axe knicking her wrists, landing on her knees. The sheriff's blood was leaking onto the ground, out from where used to be his arm.

She found her feet. Heather raised the axe, more dropping it than swinging the handle, the wood barely in her hands as it cut through the muscles and sinews of his other arm. His skin was rippling, scales and feathers and the placement of veins, visible enough to be seen in the half-light, but it wasn't fast enough to stop the blood gushing out of him. She dragged the axe back up, sweat clinging to her forehead, hands burning. Her next slice freed his head from his body.

The skull rolled away from her, picking up leaves until it *thunked* into a tree stump. Its eyelids flipped open, a glassy sheen coating Heather's mother's eyes as they stared her down.

A possum, scavenging the asphalt for roadkill, looked up at her mere feet from the road. The axe, raising to shine in the moonlight, crashing back down, blood painting the dirt and the trees and the girl. More chopped flesh than the shape of a body. It sniffed the air for a moment, then kept moving, its pale tail flicking against a fingertip that had been sent flying.

There was a bar on the far edge of the next town north, a few miles from the unofficial border of the first houses and fruit orchards. It was a few minor damages away from run-down, the roof tiles loosening and the front step almost caving under the pressure of a single footstep. The *open* sign was in neon red letters, and the jukebox had all the buttons for songs the bartender didn't like broken. It was the kind of establishment where the regulars wished they were welcome somewhere better, and the outsiders thought they could sink low enough to join their ranks.

Harvey couldn't wait to be done with his shift. It was an hour until midnight, and he figured he could weasel his way out if it stayed dead for the next half hour. It was a tuesday after all, and how many hands were needed to pour three pints?

The front door - stable-style beechwood, meant for a saloon themed diner that went bankrupt before closing - swung open, and Heather walked in. Her sweater was shredded to less than strips, revealing a dark tank top, and there was rapidly drying blood dripping from her arms and face. She stumbled up to the wooden countertop, visible exhaustion in her face as she clambered onto a bar stool. Harvey could see the red droplets beading on her cheek and staining the backpack she dragged up with her.

"Can I help you?" he asked, his voice rougher than he meant it to sound. He pushed his hands into his pockets to stop himself from anxiously wiping down the bar.

"Whiskey, please. On the rocks." She met his gaze, her eyes steady but lifeless. Something about her sent a shiver down his spine.

"You got an ID?"

She unzipped the backpack and, in a movement that felt experienced beyond her years, dropped a shotgun on the bar. The sound it made betrayed that it was loaded. Harvey felt sweat pool in the crook of his knees.

"Here," he set the glass down in front of her, watching the caramel-coloured liquid splash. "I made it a double. It's on the house."

She smiled, a gesture that was clearly both forced and practiced. "Thank you."

Harvey polished glasses three feet down the bar as Heather drained the glass, licking the ice cube before she set it back down. He turned to the sink, picking up a fresh glass still warm from the dishwasher, before dropping an ice cube into it. His hands plucked a bottle of the heavy stuff from the shelf, looking at his reflection in the mirror management had mounted behind the bar. His eyes were two different colours. He fixed it before he put the bottle back.

"Another," he set the new glass down. "Since you've drinking on me."

"Yeah," she rocked forward, visibly underage, her elbows climbing onto the bar. Her thumb swiped her bottom lip. "Is there anyone else in here tonight?"

She didn't wink. For Harvey, she didn't have to. "No," he smirked. "Just me and you and the whole-"

A bullet struck between the eyes before he could finish the sentence. Heather took a long, slow sip as she watched his body crumple, his head hitting the metal drain before he hit the ground. She counted the seconds until his forehead stopped bleeding, then again to make sure he wasn't getting back up.

"I'll take the rest of the bottle. Thanks."

∽

Heather jolted awake, faint white rays of sunlight casting onto her face while failing to warm the cracked leather bus seat she was curled up in. Her right hand flinched into her jacket, fingers brushing the leather handle of the knife strapped to her chest. She forced herself to breathe out.

There was snow on the ground outside, she could make out in the dawn, frost settling over burnt orange leaves. It was getting colder out, almost too cold for buses, most likely too cold for her jacket and assorted sweaters. Nowhere to go but further north.

She reached into the backpack that sat on the seat next to her, pulling out an almost stale bread roll and a map. She chewed absentmindedly, inking out the bus' route up the highway. At the end of the day they would reach Sweet Falls, a tourist trap that didn't know it was going out of business. It was the kind of place she could camp out in, make some money, leave behind before anyone got too used to her. Heather tucked the map and the now empty roll wrapper back into her backpack, pulled her jacket up to her ears, and let herself nod off again.

The next time she woke up, it was dark out. Knife still on her chest. The bus panted and squealed to a halt, the driver having to stand up and kick the door open. Heather was the first off, head down, walking with forced confidence. The cold air hit her hard, the same way humidity would back home, and she grit her teeth against it. It was only a ten minute walk down empty streets until she reached a motel, but it was enough for the cold to creep down her spine and start her shivering.

The clerk at the front desk couldn't have been older than fourteen, his eyes bright despite the fact that it was almost midnight. She felt old. He let her pay four nights up front, handing her a room key with an unfazed air of someone who had been trained for this exact scenario. Good.

Heather unlocked the room, walking in to peeling green wallpaper, yellowing sheets, a television with a fine layer of dust on the screen. She dead bolted the door, then pushed the dresser that could have been made of cardboard against it. There was a window across from her, curtains pulled back and blinds askew, but mimics didn't enjoy scaling walls - not if they could help it.

She dropped her backpack onto the bed, walking into the bathroom and washing her face in the tepid sink water. In the first motel she had stayed in, it had taken three showers until she stopped smelling blood, her skin scrubbed baby pink and the water long cold. She was more tired now.

Tomorrow, she would find a job at wherever was hiring. She would pour through town newspapers to see if there was anything she needed to know about. She would find a map of bus routes and plan an escape out of here, for when the time came. But tonight, there was late night television, a sandwich and a beer in her backpack, a stack of hotel magazines and local menus she could read through.

Heather changed into what she had dubbed her clean blue shirt and fresh socks, tucking the knife under one of the bed's pillows. She flicked on the television and an amber lamp, stretching her increasingly aching limbs. She walked over to the window, hands wrapping around the curtains - and there, seen through a crack in the blinds and silhouetted under a streetlight, was Tyler.

Her hand slapped over her mouth, the only thing stopping her from screaming. It was him, his shining hair and his relaxed lean anc his summer sky grey eyes staring up at her in the window, all Romeo and ready to save her. But it wasn't, was it, Heather reminded herself, biting down on the skin of her fingers. It was one of them.

For a minute, heartbeat pounding in her ears, she stood there. Her staring down at Not-Tyler, Not-Tyler staring back up at her. Neither of them moving. And then, she whisked the curtain shut and all but flung herself onto the bed.

It was following her - was still following her, all the way up from Lovely. Never moving, never acting, never speaking with its Not-Tyler voice. Just following.

Heather shivered, hard, hand curling around the hilt of the blade. Then she picked up the television remote and began flipping through the channels.

In a few hours, shortly before dawn, Heather would be asleep, spooled in blankets. The television would still be on, and Not-Tyler would still be watching her window from the street.

Rin Sangar grew up in Bicester, England, where they were raised on a steady diet of fantasy stories, Meat Loaf songs and horror films. They studied psychology in a red-bricked and swampy town in Florida, before moving to Edinburgh for a more cobblestoned and colder change of pace. They enjoy consuming horror stories in any given medium, whisky-based cocktails and spending time with their cat.

www.ingramcontent.com/pod-product-compliance
Lightning Source LLC
LaVergne TN
LVHW020439070526
838199LV00063B/4787